THE BAGHDAD CLOCK

The
Baghdad
Clock

SHAHAD AL RAWI

Translated from the Arabic by
Luke Leafgren

The Baghdad Clock

SHAHAD AL RAWI

Translated from the Arabic by
Luke Leafgren

ONEWORLD

A Oneworld Book

First published in North America, Great Britain and Australia
by Oneworld Publications, 2018

Originally published in Arabic by Dar al-Hikma, 2016

Trade paperback ISBN 978-1-78607-322-8
Hardback ISBN 978-1-78607-324-2
eBook ISBN 978-1-78607-323-5

Typeset by Siliconchips Services Ltd, UK
Printed and bound in Great Britain by Clays Ltd, St Ives plc

Oneworld Publications
10 Bloomsbury Street
London WC1B 3SR
England

Stay up to date with the latest books,
special offers, and exclusive content from
Oneworld with our newsletter

Sign up on our website
oneworld-publications.com

For Saad and Ahlam
For Shams and Shather

This translation was made possible by
a generous grant from Diwan Kufa.

The author and translator particularly wish to thank its director,
Kanan Makiya, for introducing them and supporting their
collaboration.

A cow came into her dream. Then a bicycle. Then a bridge. A military car. A cloud. Dust. A tree. A baby boy. An aeroplane. An abandoned house. A cat. A water tank. A street, a giraffe, a photograph. A song. A clock. A ship. One thing after another appeared in her dream as she got ready to weave a new one.

The cow became bored and moved on. So did a sheep. Then a horse. Then the bicycle and all the other things in an unending, chaotic cycle.

Is this a dream?

I entered her dream. I rode the bicycle and chased after the other things, driving them all out of her head. I cleaned up her dream, left the clock on the wall, and departed.

I shared her dreams because I do not dream at all. I do not know why people do it. What is this need of theirs to dream?

Book I

A Childhood of Obvious Things

1

Before she finished her story, I cut her off and got up from my seat. I went over to my mother and asked, 'Mama, why aren't my eyes green like Nadia's?'

'When you grow up, you'll be like her.'

I sat back down next to Nadia and told her, 'When I grow up, my eyes will be green.'

'They're not going to change. Because your mother – her eyes aren't green!'

'But I'm taller than you.'

She straightened up to her full height. I stood beside her and as I put my shoulder up against hers, I asked her mother, 'Who's taller?'

'You are,' her mother said.

We sat back down on the ground. I began to like her; she began to like me. I told her about my grandmother's house far away, and she asked, 'Why do you love your grandmother?'

'Because I'm her daughter,' I said.

She burst out laughing, not believing what I said but not knowing what to say. When it was time to go to sleep, she lay beside me on the rug we had brought with us from home. Her mother helped take off her black shoes and her long white socks and then covered us both up. She dimmed the lantern and moved it further away.

Before I closed my eyes, I saw Nadia smiling as she slept. Her lips moved slowly, as though she were talking to herself.

Surprised, I moved closer until my face was right in front of hers. I could see colourful phantoms moving around her forehead. I had never seen anything like these visions before. They appeared, disappeared, and then came back. I was seeing her dreams. This was the first time in my life I had entered someone's dreams.

At that moment, she began dreaming of me.

She took me by the hand and flew with me high above the old houses of Baghdad. We kept rising, climbing higher and higher until we became small as bees that vanished into thin air.

2

On the second night, we arrived at the shelter with our families just before the sun went down. Before going inside, we began playing together on the small staircase that led inside. I jumped down to the ground from the second step. Nadia went up and jumped from the third step, so I did the same. She stood on the edge of the fourth step and hesitated. She changed her mind and came back down, unable to jump from such a height. The boys who were playing near the door came over. They went up the stairs, one after the other, and began jumping down and laughing together.

While this was going on, the siren began wailing. I did not like its sound; no one did. I took Nadia's hand, and we hurried over to where our mothers were sitting. Her foot knocked over the big lantern on the floor in the middle of the shelter, breaking the glass. Oil flowed out onto the tiles and the flame took several big steps across the wet floor. We froze in the dark while the blaze of light moved our shadows on the cement wall behind us.

After a while, we heard the intense bombardment that followed the siren, violent explosions that came closer, little by little, and then began moving away. Once again, they approached and receded. The ground surged beneath us like a flimsy rug. All this time, our mothers kept saying prayers and reciting suras from the Qur'an.

I was thinking about disappearing from this world. I got up and walked over to my mother in the darkness. 'Mama?'

'Yes, my love.'

'Do you know what I want from you?'

'What do you want?'

'I don't want to be here in this world.'

Before I returned to my place, someone struck a match to light a cigarette. I saw my shadow dance on the wall. It grew bigger and spread over the ceiling of the shelter and then vanished. I stood still, thinking about my shadow. Where did it go this time? How do our shadows disappear out of this life? Am I actually just a shadow of myself?

My spirit lives in that shadow, and it departs with it because it does not like being here in this world.

I kept wishing someone would light another match so that my shadow would come back and I could talk to it. I wanted to ask, 'How are you able to disappear so we no longer see you?' But I remembered that shadows do not have voices, and I returned to my spot, slowly edging towards Nadia. It was so dark I could not see her, but I knew she was there.

The planes went away. Fear departed with them, and then it was time to sleep. I stretched out on our small rug with its colourful lines. Nadia squeezed herself next to me and fell asleep. The cold ground gnawed at our bones. My mother put a heavy blanket over our bodies and tucked in our feet. Then I felt warm.

I did not sleep that night either. I was watching Nadia's dreams. It is a fun game to watch someone's dreams when they are deep in sleep. In the morning, I told her about the dreams. She did not like that and said, 'How horrible! Why are you spying on my dreams?'

'Because I don't know how to dream.'

Many times in my life I tried to copy her beautiful dreams and insert them into my own sleep, but I always failed. I had to be content with watching these dreams of hers, and when I found them upsetting, I would clean out her head and banish the things she did not like.

I got to know Nadia in the belly of this shelter that looked like a big concrete whale. A damp place fortified against the war, our fantasies flitted across the walls. We spent more than twenty nights in the shelter, that January in 1991 when the Baghdad sky blazed with planes and rockets. And during those long weeks we lived through fear, cold and hunger, sharing our hopes and dreams. We did not know at the time what was happening around us. We did not understand then what the war meant.

Once, before we sat down on our rug, Uncle Shawkat walked over to us, smiling. He used to smile like that all the time. He gave Nadia a light pinch on the ear. He took her left wrist and used his teeth to leave the impression of a small watch on her skin. Then he took my left hand and did the same to me. His wife, Baji Nadira, came up and said to him, 'Don't do that!'

Baji Nadira kissed us both tenderly and apologised. We smiled at her, and at the same time, we were looking at the watches that gradually disappeared. Uncle Shawkat went back to his place with a group of men gathered around a small radio that was broadcasting distant whispers. His wife went and sat between my mother and Nadia's.

After a while, many women went over to join them, talking about the war. Some young girls came and sat with us. I remember Marwa, Baydaa, Wijdan, Rita and Mala'ika, which means 'angel', but whom we called 'devil' for no good reason.

'I'm not a devil!'

'Yes, you are!'

Mala'ika started crying and went to sit close to her mother, pointing at us and saying things we could not hear.

Nadia and I got up and explored the different corners of the shelter. We counted the faces in the light of the lantern, wanting to know these people who lived around our neighbourhood. Here was Umm Rita, as Rita's mother was called. Here was Abu Manaf, taking his nickname from his son Manaf, as well as Manaf's sister Manal and his little brother Ghassan, asleep on his mother's lap. Here was Umm Marwa, and Marwa's brother Marwan. Here was Hind, and over there her father and mother. Nizar and his father and mother. Mayada and her family. Umm Ali and her grown-up daughters. (Umm Ali did not have a younger daughter who sat with us.) These people lived with Umm Salli. Here was Wijdan, along with her mother and sisters. There was Farouq and his mother and father. Here was Umm Mala'ika, whose actual name was Haifa, and here was Abu Mala'ika, whose name was Osama, and Mala'ika's grandfather too. As for her grandmother, she covered her face with a black abaya and slept all the time. Here was Ahmad and his mother; his father was no longer with us because he was a martyr.

3

In my imagination, I took the people I saw in the shelter back to their houses on our street. I organised the houses in straight lines and used them to draw a big ship that resembled the neighbourhood where we were born. Then I drew white smoke rising slowly towards the clouds.

I got to know all the houses. I knew the fathers, mothers, sons and daughters. In my mind, the neighbourhood became a geometric world of lines, squares and rectangles. Someone had only to ask me about one and I would close my eyes and say, 'It's the fourth house in that direction.'

After that, the neighbourhood was no longer what I had imagined it to be: a vast, unlimited space. It had become small and clearly defined. When we get to know things, they are no longer as big as they used to be. I will prove it to you with an example. When you start school and learn about the size of galaxies, you begin to see Planet Earth as a little ball. Same thing with the moon and the sun: you begin to see them as small things, right? Big things are those we imagine before we know their limits.

Have I made this idea clear? Some ideas need to be explained since we think them up by ourselves to start with. At first, the idea is born in our imagination, and when we want to talk about it with others, we do not know how to make them understand it perfectly like we do. So we need to explain it using simple examples. For instance, take a man who wants to make a bicycle. Let us suppose that he is the

first person ever to make a bicycle. It starts with this idea
born in his head. Then he draws it and says to himself, 'If
this bicycle doesn't move, it will fall over.' He explains it to
his friend, but his friend does not understand and replies,
'I'm standing in one place, and I'm not falling down. Listen,
friend, I don't need to move in order to stay upright.' The
one making the bicycle says, 'That's true, but are you able
to make a wheel stand up without falling? Wheels don't fall
when they move.' His friend replies, 'Ah! Now I understand
what you're thinking.' That is why we always need to clarify
our ideas to others.

When the war ended, we no longer went to the shelter
every evening. I began spending time at Nadia's house,
or she would come to ours, and we would play together.
Sometimes we would go out into the street by ourselves,
but we would not go far. We would count the houses one
by one and scribble on the walls with chalk. We drew big
white faces and used different colours to draw small bodies
and fingers. We drew Uncle Shawkat sitting on the sofa and
wearing glasses. Baji Nadira sat next to him, laughing. Over
their heads we drew a small sparrow without a cage. We
drew Umm Rita with her broken arm in a sling. We drew
the cat from Umm Manaf's house looking out at us. We drew
Ahmad's father flying among the clouds, even though we had
never seen him before.

One day in April, most likely a Friday, I went with my
parents to Al-Zawra Park. Nadia's family was with us. So was
Baydaa and her mother, but I do not remember if her father
was there or not. We sat on the grass and ate the food we
had brought from home. After a while, we left our families
sitting there, and the three of us ran among the trees, trying
to catch ladybirds. When we got close to the zoo, we threw
some food to the hungry giraffes who lived in big cages.

Baydaa pointed to a tall, round building and said, 'That's the Zawra Tower.'

'But it's smaller than the Ma'mun Tower,' I said.

Nadia, very sure of what she was saying, replied, 'The Ma'mun Tower gets bigger every day.'

During the holiday after Ramadan, Nadia went to visit her mother's sister and I went to visit my father's sister. When Nadia came back, she told me stories she had heard from her aunt and I told her stories I had made up.

When winter came, it started raining and we went to school. I raised my hand and said to the teacher, 'Ma'am, I would like to sit next to Nadia.'

'Nadia with the green eyes?' the teacher asked.

'Yes, ma'am. She's my friend, and when I grow up, my eyes are going to be green like hers.'

The teacher laughed, but I did not. Sometimes, teachers laugh for no reason. I went and sat at Nadia's desk, which was close to the window where cold air was coming in. I rubbed my hands together quickly because of the cold, and Nadia did the same. I rubbed out the mistakes I made during the dictation using Nadia's colourful erasers, and every time I used them to erase the letters that were wrong, they gave off a smell I liked. I like making mistakes very much because I get to rub them out.

Nadia always forgets things, and I always remember. Sometimes, when she gets distracted, I tell her, 'Pay attention!' And when I start dozing at our desk, she tells me, 'Don't fall asleep!'

Once, in November, when I wanted to disappear because it was so cold, we left school to go home and Nadia came across a blind cat on the pavement. Small and white, it was wet and shivering from the cold. Nadia handed me her book bag and carried the cat against her chest.

As for how we knew it was blind, that is not complicated. When you find a small cat and move your finger in front of its eyes, if it does not move its head back and forth, that means it cannot see.

We built a small hut for it in the yard under the olive tree and left it sleeping there. Nadia's mother was watching us from the window; she called to us and we went inside.

'What are you doing in the yard when it's so cold out?'

'We found a kitten that's going to die from the cold!'

She gave us some food for our cat, which we put in front of it and waited. We were shivering from the cold. The cat smelled the food and turned its face away. We pushed the dish close to its mouth again, but it did not eat anything.

After a while, my mother came looking for me and found me playing in Nadia's yard. She was afraid because I was late getting home. I was surprised. How did my mother know I was late?

I did not know anything about time except for seven-thirty when the school bell rang for the start of classes. I also knew one o'clock, when it rang a second time for the end of classes and we left to go home. There was another time that I did not know, a very long time that began at one in the afternoon and went until seven-thirty in the morning. Grown-ups use other times that we don't know about.

My mother was angry and gripped my hand. It was the first time I had ever been afraid of my mother, and I started to cry. Nadia ran to catch up with us, and when she saw my tears, she started crying too. Umm Manaf was standing in her doorway, watching. Umm Manaf always stood in the her doorway watching the neighbours. Even when I went to school in the morning I would see her standing there, watching people.

My mother was embarrassed by the situation. We went inside our house, and the first thing I did was change my clothes. After lunch, my mother took me back to Nadia's house and left me there. Nadia and I played in her yard until evening. We brought lots of rags and some pieces of thick cardboard to put over the blind cat's hut. 'Go to sleep!' we told it, and it did.

That night, Nadia dreamed that I became a white cat. I was wet and shivered from the cold. In the morning, she discovered that our cat had vanished from the small house we had built for it the day before. She never found it again.

How is it possible for a small blind cat to run away in the dark? Do you believe me when I tell you that such a thing happened to us?

I closed my eyes in order to see the world like the blind cat. I saw an enormous empty space surrounded by a thin yellow border. Inside, visions of dim light appeared in circles that started small but then grew bigger and bigger until they disappeared. The blind cat lived in a world of circles that got bigger and bigger and then disappeared.

Back then, Nadia's dreams resembled the moving circles. Every time she found herself in trouble, standing in some high place where she could not take a step, she would call her mother as loudly as she could, but her mother would not hear. She would look at the deep chasms around her. She would fall in, but she would not die.

In some of her dreams, her green eyes changed colour. She liked the colour of her eyes very much and was upset when they changed. Every morning when she woke up, she would go to the mirror to check that they were green, just as they had been before she went to bed. Then she would laugh at herself.

I entered her dreams, like I told you at the beginning. I lived in them without anyone seeing me. Even if I called out to someone at the top of my voice, or I grabbed their hand, they would not see me. Only once, something happened that I did not expect. Devil Mala'ika was in one of the dreams, sitting next to the wall around her house. When I went up to her, she slapped my cheek, though I did not feel any pain.

When I try to remember that time, what comes back are the days of bitter cold, or the times when it rained. As for the summer, what I remember are the nights we slept on the roof. Those nights have all collapsed into a single night, a time I counted the distant stars, and when I went to sleep, the stars fell into the yard. That is why the rain will appear so frequently in my stories, and it is as though the burning summer sun was never there at all.

At my grandmother's house far away, the stars were closer than they were at home. We went there eight days before the war began. That was also in January 1991. We were afraid of the war, and my father decided that we would go there and be safe from the rockets because my grandmother did not fear the war, and the war took no notice of her.

My grandmother's house was big. It was surrounded by tall trees with little canals running between them where green frogs jumped. Two white ducks swam in the small pond behind the fence, followed by their four or five ducklings. I do not remember exactly how many ducklings there were, but I do remember they walked on the water and did not get wet.

A grey cat sat by the edge of the pond. It was not blind or wet. It watched the ducklings and lapped the cold water with its tongue. When I got close, it ran away and disappeared among the trees.

Even when it was very cold out, my grandmother would get up each day at dawn and pray because God could see her as she prayed in the dark. Grandmother would speak to the stars, and when the sun came up behind her four palm trees, she would come into the kitchen and make me breakfast. Her breakfasts were delicious. I have not had such food anywhere else in my entire life.

Grandmother loved me. She spoiled me and took good care of me. I used to wish she was my mother, and I was delighted when she told me a secret that has remained between us until now: 'I carried you in this tummy of mine before it gave birth to your mother.'

At night, I shared her wide bed, a bed which swam with us through space. I did not see her dreams. My grandmother did not dream, and her eyes were not green. When she dozed off with her hand under her cheek, she neither smiled nor spoke to herself. She just slept so that stars might enter the window and encircle the picture of my grandfather, hanging on the wall to guard us from thieves. I did not know my grandfather, and he did not know me. All the same, I loved him and wished that we could see each other. He had been there in that picture for a long time, looking at us without saying a single word. The first time I saw his picture, I asked Grandmother, 'Who's that?' She replied, 'That's Harun al-Rashid,' which made my aunt laugh, as well as my father and my mother. I did not laugh. After a while, my father said to me, 'It's your grandfather.'

Far from the house, on the opposite side of the garden, there were big wooden wheels called *norias* that took water from the river and poured it into the canals. The *norias* were close to the river, and so was the house, but even so, I could not see the river. At night, the smell of small fish came to me from the water, along with the songs of people immersed in the depths of time.

Nadia had never seen the river before either. Once, we were running in the inner courtyard of the school, and she sang: '*I crossed the Shutt for you.*'

Our friend Marwa came over and told us, '*Shutt* is another name for the river.'

Some days later, Nadia went with her family to visit relatives on the eastern side of the Tigris River. Their car crossed the river, and Nadia saw a mangled bridge, killed by aeroplanes in the war. She saw the waves, the fish and the small boats. She smelled the air of the river and loved it. That night, she dreamed that her book bag fell into the water. The waves took it far away and a white bird came and stole it.

In the schoolyard, Marwa said, 'Liar! Birds don't steal book bags because they don't read or write.'

'Nadia's not a liar! I saw that in her dream too.'

'How did you see her dream? You're a liar like her.'

4

In our fourth year at school, I grew tall, taller than Nadia, but my eyes were not green. They stayed just like they were when I was small. My mother had not been lying at that time. It is just that I got big and left them as they were; I had simply changed my mind. I did not want my eyes to be green. Green eyes see the world just like the rest of us. Nadia did not see everything as green: I was not green; our house was not green; the sky was not green. But the trees and the grass were green.

I was taller than Nadia. I see things from far away, and the things I do not see I imagine. If you want the truth, I like the things I imagine better than the things I see. When I decided one day to see the River Tigris, I climbed the stairs of the house to the roof because the river was far away, and when we climb up on the roof of the house, we see distant things. I stood on the water tank that was on the roof over the second floor. I turned in all directions, but I did not see the Tigris or any other river. I saw many bridges, buildings, tall trees, and birds circling in the sky.

Before I forget, let me describe for you what else I saw that evening. I saw an enormous, unending ocean of space. In this gigantic ocean of horizons that stretched far under the light of the setting sun, I saw our neighbourhood as though it were a ship anchored along the shore, a gigantic ship with the Ma'mun Tower in the middle like its tall sail. The Baghdad Clock looked like an anchor thrown on the harbour quay, and the Zawra Tower was like the ship's bridge, where the captain steered.

I thought to myself, 'One day, when this ship sets off, the enormous engine will groan into life; it will puff its white steam into the sky, and its whistle will sound far and wide. Everyone will climb aboard for a long journey towards the Isle of Safety, towards harbours no one has ever reached before. This ship will voyage out, further and further, until all trace of it is lost in the thick fog of forgetfulness.'

I forgot to tell you about something else. Not too long after that, when I was leaving school after classes were over one day in February, I heard music echoing through the sky, music that I imagine most of you heard on the television or radio in those days: '*Bum, ba bum bum … bum, ba bum bum.*'

Do you remember it? I do. I don't know how old you are now, but if you were in Baghdad when the clock opened in 1994, you would remember it. Everyone who was in Baghdad in 1994 remembers the clock and its music.

A week or so later, we went on a school trip to the museum surrounding the new Baghdad Clock. We toured the halls and gardens. Then they took us inside, where we saw clean glass cases displaying gifts that people had presented to the president of the Republic. They had given him traditional swords, old rifles, and decorated panels with poems about his life. We saw stone reliefs and small clay seals that told stories about the ancient people who lived in Iraq thousands of years before us.

Someone had drawn a big picture of the president and, alongside it, an even bigger picture of Harun al-Rashid. I said to the teacher, 'Harun al-Rashid is my grandfather.'

'I know,' my teacher replied. 'He looks like you.' She burst out laughing as though she would die.

Some poor women, who did not have anything to give the president as a gift, had cut off their braids, written their names on them, and put them in the museum. I do not know what the president does with women's braids.

The clock struck ten o'clock, and this time I heard the words of its patriotic song: '*With you, Saddam, the folk have made their pact; you've seen their lofty sacrifice.*'

In the garden at the front, under the clock that read 10:10, we stood in a single row for a photograph to commemorate the occasion. That picture remains the only one I have of us all gathered together in one place: me, Nadia, Ahmad, Farouq, Baydaa, Marwa, Wijdan, Rita and Manaf, with the rest of the students in our class.

On the right of the picture, Mrs Najah stood with her blonde hair and her red shirt. She put her hand on my shoulder and smiled for the camera. I loved Mrs Najah so much. And I liked it that she always put her hand on my shoulder. She was a good teacher who loved us all and laughed with us. When her husband drove up in a white car and waited for her at the door of the school, wearing his pilot's uniform, we greeted him, and he would laugh with us too.

Nadia dreamed she was running in the garden of the Baghdad Clock. She tripped and fell on the grass, cutting her leg. Ahmad came over to her, took a handkerchief out of his pocket, and sat down to press the handkerchief against the wound. Was that a dream, or was it an actual event that I have forgotten?

Another day in February, we were going to school, and we saw Farouq. He was wearing jeans, a white shirt and grey shoes, and he was not carrying his book bag. This image of him was somewhat strange. He told us he was taking that day as a holiday from school, and that his father was travelling far away.

A little later, Ahmad came up on his bicycle, smiling and singing to himself. He turned to Nadia and said, 'I have a cat with green eyes.'

'Liar! You do not.'

Nadia took a piece of chalk out of her bag and wrote on the wall of the school in the large, carefully formed letters they taught us in class. 'Ahmad stole our cat.'

Many years from now, Nadia and I will pass by this place, next to that very wall. We will read the name Ahmad and laugh at the memory. The words we wrote with chalk on the wall of the school will remain there forever so that we might remember them and laugh.

On that same day, Mrs Najah came in and handed out copies of our class photo taken in front of the Baghdad Clock. We made fun of Marwa because she appeared behind Ahmad's shoulder like Yasmina in the television series, *Sinbad*. In this picture, we discovered that the clock was smiling at us. Baydaa said, 'It's laughing at us,' and Mrs Najah laughed too.

5

At night before I fell to sleep, I thought about the Baghdad Clock. How did it stand there by itself in the dark without being afraid? I imagined it resting its head on its shoulder and dozing off. But which way would it bend to sleep? When did it wake up? Did it feel tired like us? Did it get any time off?

My parents had gone to sleep and all the lights in the house were off. I got up out of bed, put on my mother's long coat from the hall cupboard and walked on tiptoes to the front gate. A white cat – not the blind, wet one – beat me to it and leaped over it onto the pavement. I ignored the cat, slowly opened the gate, and went out into the street.

When I got to the end of the street, I heard a car approaching. Its headlights shot out in front. I immediately pressed myself against the wall of the shop. The car passed by me and turned into the street that ran parallel to our school, the same street where Nadia and I found the blind, wet cat.

A few moments later, the world had fallen back into a deep silence. I went in the direction of the main street on the other side and walked towards the clock.

Halfway there, I hesitated and decided to return home and sleep. I do not know why I then continued on my way, all alone in the darkness. Sometimes we decide on something but do precisely the opposite.

I arrived at the clock, which was prettier at night than it was during the day. When you go around it and look at it from every side, you can see that it is actually not one clock, but rather four clocks, each one facing in a different direction. I do not know why it was not called the Baghdad Clocks, seeing as they had put a big lamp on the ground in front of each one of the four.

The short hand was pointing at one, and the long hand at nine. In that moment, Nadia was dreaming. She usually dreamed at that time of the night. I wanted to carry the clock and put it in her dream, but her dream was short and the clock was tall.

I walked close to the building, which formed an eight-pointed star. The tall tower, which we saw from afar, stood atop it. I drew back and sat on the ground behind the big lamps illuminating the tower.

'Tick, tock, tick, tock, tick, tock…'

What is the use of time if a person does not hear the sound of the swinging pendulum? I used to like talking to this thin object that would take half a step back and then half a step forward. That is all it needed to be happy.

I said to myself, 'Why does it count the small seconds that people have no use for?' Then I asked it, 'Who cares about the seconds at this time of the night, when people are asleep? Don't you get tired?'

'One day I'll get tired, and then I'll stop forever.'

'When will that be?'

'When there is no longer a ship anchored in this wide ocean of darkness.'

The hour hand remained fixed at one, and the minute hand pointed at twelve. I got up and brushed bits of wet grass off my clothes. Turning around, I ran towards the main street, pursued by the faint lights of a distant car. The car took a sudden turn to the left, and darkness once again filled the world. I saw a soldier on guard duty carrying a rifle, but he was looking the other way and did not see me.

While I was on my way back, I saw in front of me the prow of an enormous ship with the Ma'mun Tower in the middle, like a mast with its sails furled. I went through a small opening on the side of the ship, wandering through dark passageways as I looked for the shortest path to the side facing the water. The sound of crashing waves reached me, and I was struck with an intense dizziness that nearly made me lose my balance and fall down. I really heard waves, and everyone has to believe me when I tell them about my journey inside the ship.

I am not lying. I will tell you what I saw, or what I imagined. When I was wandering through the ship, I thought to myself, 'Should I tell them what I was thinking?' Because most people only believe things that come into their own minds, and they do not know things that have not occurred to them.

The captain arrived, half-asleep at that hour. He asked, 'What are you doing here at a time like this?'

'I want to ride the ship and travel far away.'

'But you were born on it, and if you want to travel, you have to get off.'

After that, he started walking back to his cabin to sleep. I ran after him and called out, 'Who are you? I've never seen you in the neighbourhood before, and I don't know you personally, even though I've met all the people around here.'

He gestured that I should wait and entered his cabin. Re-emerging with a teapot, he poured us each a small cup. Then he sat on a small bench, looked into my face, and said, 'Where are we right now?'

'We're on the deck of the ship,' I replied.

'Is there a ship without a captain?'

'I don't know.'

'Is there a car that moves without a driver?'

'No.'

'I'm the driver,' he said. 'I'm the one who guides this ship.'

'But this ship doesn't move.'

He laughed. 'I'm the driver of the ship that doesn't move. My sole duty is to keep it from moving.'

'What's the use of a ship that doesn't move?'

He drank his tea and poured himself another cup. 'It's stopped here so that the travellers can get off.'

'And where will you go if everyone gets off?'

He stood up with his tea and leaned against the rail, looking off into the unending darkness of the ocean. He spoke, as though talking to someone else: 'Listen, my dear. The ship is an idea in your head, and I am an idea in the head of the ship. Small ideas usually have delicate wings, and when they lose their value on the earth, they fly up into space. The world we live in is just an idea made by the imagination of an inventive creator, and when he found it to be complicated, he began explaining it by means of other, smaller ideas. And so, after millions of years, the sky is filled with ideas that fly around on delicate wings. Everything our eyes touch is just an idea. There's nothing real about reality. We are prisoners of our imaginations, and our experiences in the world of reality consist only of ideas. All of existence is an assembly of ideas. That is the sole truth. Don't believe anything else. And don't tell anyone, because people only believe things that come independently to their minds. Yet they don't know where the mind is to be found. There's never a day when they ask themselves, "Do I actually possess a thing called the mind? What is it shaped like? What's its colour?" The mind, my little one, is another idea. A complicated idea made of other ideas as though they were real.'

I did not understand the captain's words, but he was telling me the truth. I instinctively know when people are telling the truth. Sometimes there are things we do not understand, and we know their meaning, not through words but rather, the meaning is already inside us before others talk to us about it. Some meanings exist inside us but are sleeping. Then words that we understand come and wake them up.

Often, when I am alone in bed before I fall asleep, I say to myself, 'Why don't I dream like Nadia?' Then I think a little and go on to say, 'Maybe I dream too, but I don't know that I'm dreaming. Maybe I'm a long dream in the head of someone who is sleeping and doesn't wake up. Someone who's dreaming my whole life.'

Am I a dream or an idea like the captain said? What is the difference between a dream and an idea? Should I be happy if my life is only a dream in someone's head?

I left the captain without saying goodbye since his mind was elsewhere. Without turning towards me, he kept talking, looking out into the darkness of the unending ocean.

At the end of a long passageway, I saw the shelter where we had slept to escape the war in January 1991. I thought about going inside, but I gave up that idea. I was afraid, and my heart pounded violently.

I ran towards our street. Pushing open our gate, I quietly entered the house on tiptoes. The white cat jumped in front of me a second time and disappeared among the dense trees in the far corner of the garden. I left the front door half open, climbed the stairs to my room, and sat on my bed. I was guiding the ship into the distance like a courageous captain, braving rainstorms and violent winds that blasted the sails. When the sun rose and shone through the window, the storms had blown themselves out, the waves had retreated and the ship had come safe to harbour – all thanks to the guidance of the wise captain.

6

The spring air is refreshing, and the days are growing slightly longer. We cast off our heavy clothes and feel ourselves becoming lighter. The boys come out on their bicycles, racing through the streets and happily ringing the little bells on the handlebars. Mothers and fathers head out to the gardens, and we too come out to play on the pavement.

Abu Baydaa sprays his garden with water, spreading a refreshing fragrance everywhere. Umm Rita waters the area around her front porch so the smell of the earth rises and spreads the scent of the late spring breezes over her. Like you, I love the smell of earth when raindrops fall on it. Like you, I do not know why I do.

From Umm Salli's house comes the smell of grilled meat and a dish of potatoes fried in fat, and we all feel a little hungry.

Suddenly, music bursts out from Umm Manaf's house and, moved by its rhythm, we run, forgetting our hunger. We enter a festival of colours worn by the young women as they dance to celebrate Manal's wedding. Her mother distributes traditional wedding sweets wrapped into shiny squares. The songs become louder, and perfume wafts everywhere.

My God, my God, Manal, how pretty, so pretty
Tears of joy, Manal, and hands of henna

I stand far from the little girls and thrust my small head among the bodies of the women so I can see Nadia as she dances in the middle of the garden near Manal. Everyone likes it when Nadia dances, and they clap for her. Manal draws her in and kisses her. Envy consumes my heart, and I ask myself, 'How did she learn to dance like grown-ups? Why isn't she embarrassed in front of these women? It's as though she's lost in her own world!'

All the girls applaud Nadia, and the singing grows even louder. Boys climb the wall around the house to watch Nadia, who dances on, unaware of their presence. One of them shouts out something rude. Nadia stops dancing, and the boy flees, followed by his gang of friends. Nadia and I go out of the garden. Her cheeks are red with embarrassment.

We hear a new song coming from the garden, but Nadia refuses to go back. Manal's mother comes out to stand at the gate, calling her, but Nadia runs home and does not come out again that evening.

As I have said before, I will tell you the truth. I was a little jealous of Nadia – maybe a lot – because people loved her and took an interest in her. We all like it when people care, and if nobody takes an interest in us, we do not exist. Sometimes when people ignore me, I cry. I just go to my room and cry. Then I come out and do strange things so that others pay attention to me. Do you know what these strange things are? When I remember them, I will tell you, but right now I have forgotten.

I lived my days in our own neighbourhood – its streets and alleys, its gardens and pavements – amid that enlivening air that drifted out of the gardens and over our childhood.

I drew a small boat on the wall of Uncle Shawkat's house. But I forgot to draw its sails, for in my whole life I had never seen an ocean or a sea and I had never been on a boat. I had seen the sunset from atop the water tank, like I told you, and it was like an enormous ocean that stretched very far, even further than my grandmother's house. On television I watched *Sinbad*, and I saw the ship battling the waves on the deep seas. Sinbad and Yasmina both laughing loudly, happy to reach the harbour: 'We've arrived at the floating island!'

The next day, I hid a piece of chalk in my pocket, went to Nadia, and said, 'Let's go and draw sails on the small boat.'

'I'll draw the harbour and the seagulls.'

'I'll draw the sails.'

We arrived at the wall, and as we were about to scribble on the clean wall of their house, Uncle Shawkat came out to us and grabbed us. He gave Nadia a gentle pinch on the ear and imprinted a clock deep on the skin of her wrist. It hurt a little, and Nadia was about to cry. Pain mixed with shame, and a small tear shone in her eye.

Uncle Shawkat was sad about this turn of events, which he had not expected. He took us by the hand and led us inside the house, where he wiped away Nadia's tears. Baji Nadira came up, scolding him and bending over to smile at us as she apologised. Every time we saw them together, he would bite our wrists, and she would scold him and apologise.

I do not remember – neither does Nadia, nor her family nor mine – when Uncle Shawkat and Baji Nadira came to live in that house. The houses that were born before us, and the trees that grew up before we entered the world, did not have a history that people remembered.

Their house had a low wall running between the front garden and the street. It was covered in ivy with tree branches rising above it. The main gate opened by the garage where Uncle Shawkat kept his small, yellow Volkswagen. At the end of the garage, there was an opening, tiled with mosaics, which led through a side passage and into the back garden. This is the only house that had its own smell in my memory. It is also the first house that comes to mind when I try to imagine the neighbourhood.

Baji Nadira and Uncle Shawkat were raising a pair of partridges in their back garden. Baji Nadira had brought them with her from Kurdistan. On one of the branches of the pomegranate tree hung a small cage for a nightingale, which sang every morning. It sometimes sang in the evening too, but it slept at night. Their furniture was similar to that of the other houses in the neighbourhood, except it was more spread out, so the house felt more spacious and comfortable.

On the wall that ran parallel to the dining table, there was an elegant picture of the young couple on their honeymoon at a Kurdistan holiday resort, with the Geli Ali Beg waterfall behind them. The water gushed down and carved out a small river among the rocks. This river ran through the valleys for a great long way before emptying into the River Tigris. Standing beneath Geli Ali Beg, the couple wore warm smiles that made the snow atop the mountains melt and pour forth as a song that wandered among distant valleys. Their photograph was a waterfall of memories that flowed in silence towards the infinite.

Uncle Shawkat and Baji Nadira lived in this intimate kingdom, and in the evenings they watched television together on the very sofa that Nadia and I were sitting on eating candy, after Nadia had dried her tears.

Although they had been married for many years, they did not have any children. Baji Nadira had not given birth to any daughters to play with us. Nadia and I and all the children of the neighbourhood were their children. We all went into their house and ate food that Baji Nadira made. We liked it very much, and she was happy with us. She would tell us stories in her Kurdish accent about the majestic mountains and about Mamand and his beloved, whom he stole away to live with him there for the rest of their lives. She told us about squirrels and farmers and other stories.

'There was a farmer and his son, and neither of them could hear very well. One morning, the son woke up very early and put on his work clothes. His father saw him and asked, "Are you off to plough the field, my boy?" And the son replied, "No, father. I'm off to plough the field." And the father said, "That's fine, my boy. I thought you were off to plough the field!"'

Nadia and I laughed at this delightful story. 'Another!' we said.

Baji Nadira lifted her head, looking at the ceiling to remember. 'There was a small village on the side of a big mountain called Birah Magrun. In this village there was a beautiful young woman who lived with her family. Every day she dreamed that a handsome young man came through the window to talk to her, but in the morning when she woke up, he was nowhere to be found. One day, snow fell and covered the entire ground. The young woman, whose name was Joanna, went out and climbed up the mountainside until she became tired. She sat down to think about this young man whom she saw only in her dreams. She said to herself, "I've never seen him in real life, so why don't I make his likeness out of snow?" She began gathering the snow around her until there was a large enough pile, and then she sat down and used it to make the young man of her dreams. After an hour, she had created the likeness of a friend with big eyes and blond hair, exactly as she saw him in her dreams. She stood in front of him, looking into his eyes. Then he spoke: "I love you!" Joanna was embarrassed, and her cheeks flushed red.

'"What's your name?" she asked.

'"My name is Mando."

'"Why are you so thin?"

'"Because I'm hungry."

'She smiled at him and said, "I'll go home and bring you something to eat." He smiled and thanked her. Joanna hurried through the snow towards the house, but she got lost along the way because the snow had covered her tracks. Meanwhile, the sun came out from behind the clouds. When Joanna reached the house, she got some food and ran back to where she had left her friend. She was happy with the food she was bringing him.

'But she didn't find any trace of Mando because the sun's heat had melted him. Joanna was very sad and began to cry. She threw the food on the ground, and sparrows came to eat it. And ever since that day, Joanna has got up each morning to bring food to throw to the sparrows in that same place. This beautiful young woman didn't like the sun because it had taken Mando from her. One day, when she was carrying food out to the sparrows, she saw the sun dip close to the mountainside, and she asked, "Why did you take Mando, Mrs Sun?" The sun replied, "I didn't take Mando. He loved you so much that he melted from love and became a creek."'

Nadia and I were sad for Joanna and Mando, and Baji Nadira was sad with us. But she told us, 'Some other time I'll tell you the happy ending for this young woman, who meets the young man of her dreams again.'

In later years, Uncle Shawkat's appearance was no longer elegant like it was when I was little, when he had his new suit and his white shirt with a blue tie over it. He stopped caring about his clothing. Even his tie became old and faded. He no longer smiled at us very often, and when we greeted him, he would return the greeting coldly, without looking at our faces.

Baji Nadira left her job and kept busy by looking after her house and her husband. She was especially eager to keep their front door clean, as well as the pavement and the windows, and she was anxious about the sheds and birdcages in their garden. I loved her Kurdish clothing for its beautiful colours; I loved her dances and her Kurdish songs at celebrations.

> *Nargus! Owei, narcissus, so lovely and so high*
> *Owei, nargus! The mountaintop, the blooming narcissus*

Early one morning, a few days after Nadia and I had been inside their house, Baji woke up, packed a suitcase and travelled to her family in their mountain village. No news came of her at all after that visit, and when someone in the neighbourhood asked Uncle Shawkat the reason for her disappearance, he sometimes said she was sick, and sometimes that her mother had died. As time went on, he learned to live by himself, and people got used to forgetting about Baji Nadira.

To be honest, it is not that people forgot her, but rather they got used to forgetting her absence. It was not that they forgot her as a person. There are people in the neighbourhood – indeed, in every place around the world – about whom forgetting means that we remember their absence, and this absence takes the place of their presence in our lives. Baji Nadira was one of those whom it was impossible to forget. Only a few days ago, we even dreamed she told us a new story that I will share with you when the time is right.

7

Even though I liked my school during the day, I was afraid of its ghosts at night. All the children were afraid of the school building during the night-time. During the day, they feared the head teacher.

One night, towards the end of June, we were playing in the light of a street lamp in our street. We were about to go home when Baydaa said, 'Come on! Let's go to the school and climb the wall.' At first, this idea seemed strange to us, but Nadia said, 'Yes, let's do it! We'll go to where the boys are playing football, and we'll tell them that the results of the national aptitude test have been hanging on the noticeboard outside the head teacher's office since this afternoon. Then we'll watch them climb the wall, and we'll run away and leave them there!'

The boys could not believe their ears when we asked them to perform this heroic task for us. They immediately left their small playing field and ran ahead of us. One after another, they climbed over the wall and jumped down inside the dark school building. We fled and left them there, nearly dying of laughter. However, these wicked boys spoiled our fun, for after a short while, they returned, having discovered our trick. Carrying papers with grades from an old exam that they had taken from the board, they told us, 'Here are the results of the test!'

We were all astonished to find that our lie had actually been the truth, and the trick was turned against us. We began begging them to tell us what was on the papers. 'They're just

blank pages!' we said, but they insisted that they were the
test results. To prove it, they told me, 'You have to repeat
English.' They told Nadia, 'You failed every subject and will
repeat the year!' To Baydaa, they said, 'Congratulations,
smarty! You passed!' And they told Marwa, 'Your results
haven't come out yet.'

We kept begging them to see the results with our own eyes,
but they absolutely refused and ended up running away with
the papers. We went home, but anxiety prevented us from
sleeping that whole long night. Dear God, was it true that
I had failed English? I tried to recall the questions and my
answers, but my memory was all jumbled up, and I forgot
everything about the test. I even forgot if I had been tested
in all the subjects, even though I had never missed a day of
school in my entire life.

Every time fear filled my heart, I would tell myself, 'They're
lying! I didn't forget. I'm good at every subject, especially
English. I memorised the book cover to cover! How could I
have failed such an easy subject? And how could Nadia have
failed everything when she's one of the smartest students in
the school? Why hadn't Marwa's results appeared if these
were the national tests?'

I wanted to get up from my bed and go out into the street.
I was choking on this atmosphere of fear that prevented me
from sleeping. It was a time when the electricity had gone
out, which happened a lot in those days. I got up and went to
the kitchen, where I opened the refrigerator and drank a lot
of water. When I went back to bed, I fell asleep immediately
without another thought about the results.

Nadia knocked on the door of our house very early the next
morning, wearing her school uniform. She said to my mother,
'The results have come out, and we have to go and get them.'
My mother replied, 'You're dreaming! Test results don't come

out at a time like this.' I was listening to their conversation from behind the door, and when Nadia ran off, I went back to sleep. But my mother was not able to go back to sleep. She started making breakfast for us, and before waking me, she went to the school herself and came back, calling, 'Get up, sleepyhead! You've passed with an average of ninety-three per cent!' In that moment, I thought she was joking, but after I'd made sure, I jumped from the bed into her arms and kissed her face. Then my father woke up and kissed me. This was the first time my father had kissed me on the occasion of receiving test results without also picking me up and spinning me around with joy. I had grown bigger, and his hands were weak. Why, Dad? I am not grown up yet. Even though I am bigger, I want you to pick me up and spin me around the room. I want you to throw me in the air, my entire life floating up, waiting for your hands to catch me and keep me from hitting the floor. I was so angry with you but did not say so at the time. I was too embarrassed to say that in front of you since you considered me to have grown up. In your hands, Dad, I am little even when I am thirty years old. I am always small and suspended in mid-air between your outstretched arms.

I had passed, Nadia had passed, and so had Baydaa and Marwa. We met in Baydaa's garden and made fun of the boys who were still sleeping at this late hour and did not know that the test results had actually come out. After a while, we went out and knocked on Ahmad's door and told him, 'We've passed! As for you, go to school, and you'll see who failed English, smarty-pants.' We did that with Farouq, Nizar, Manaf and the rest of the boys. An hour later, the neighbourhood was filled with joy. Everyone had passed.

That was a special day I will never forget. Sadly, joy and sorrow were joined together that day, and the happiness in our neighbourhood did not last long. That very day, after

Nizar had received his exam results, a big black Chevrolet stopped at the door of their house, one that we would get used to seeing later on. That was the moment they left their home and emigrated from Iraq. We would never see them again.

I did not know then what it meant for a family to emigrate and leave the neighbourhood. We were not used to anything like that. The sanctions were not as severe as they would be in the coming years.

The day before, I had happened to hear my mother talking with Nadia's mother about the sanctions, but I had not paid close attention. I had often heard the word 'sanctions' in those days, and I hated it. On account of this word alone, it was necessary to bear with grown-ups' moods and not ask too many questions. Because of the sanctions, my mother was deprived of the comfort she was accustomed to and began complaining of boredom. We could not ask her for anything, not even something simple that cost only a word. Imagine, a single word making my mother tired! My father became very quiet. He would drift off and contemplate the ceiling as though it was the very first time he had seen a fan. We went out only rarely. We did not go to Lake Habbaniyah that summer, and we did not go on long drives.

The black car drove away. Abu Nizar's house remained empty, and soon it was covered with dust. The trees drooped. A long iron chain had been wrapped around their front gate, making it look sad. The family had actually emigrated, and from the trees and the downcast walls alone, it was easy to see that they were not coming back.

In the course of just a few days, the house had become old, with frightening ghosts moving about inside it. We even became afraid to approach it. The cats, however, were not afraid, and they jumped up on the outer wall and then down inside. They wandered freely through the house. Umm Nizar's house had become a home for ghosts and stray cats.

During that summer holiday, Umm Nizar's family was not the only one that left the neighbourhood. Umm Ali and Umm Salli emigrated too, followed by Umm Rita's household. The scene of tears and farewells became normal. Each time, we would stand there saying goodbye to a friend who was moving away with her family. We did not have the slightest hope that we would see her again.

'It's death in another form,' said my mother. 'Someone in your life disappears, and you don't have any hope of meeting them again. The way I see it, that means that each of you, from the point of view of the other, has died.' My mother always made things more complicated. For her, everything was connected to death.

Death is the long absence after which there is no hope of reunion. The deceased has gone to paradise, but for the one who emigrates from their country, hell follows close behind.

At first, the mothers would sit in the doorways at the terrible hour of sadness whenever a family left their house to embark on that long journey. They would exchange stories about these neighbours who were leaving, from their first day in the street until the last moment when they got into the car. But then we became used to it.

When we saw a family getting into the big black Chevrolet, the suitcases stacked on top made it clear they were emigrating. Everyone stood around to bid them farewell, and that was it. People quickly adapt themselves to sad things when they are repeated and become a natural, expected event. It is the things we do not expect that produce extreme sadness. Therefore, the sadness was most intense at the beginning, when the first families left. That does not mean we did not feel sad when we passed by abandoned houses and

remembered the families who used to live there. Precisely
the opposite. The sorrow then would be deeper and more
painful, and there are even more tears than at the moment
of departure itself. Not because we have lost people whom
we love, but we are pained at the sight of their beautiful
houses, which blur like dark forests in the smoke.

It was in October, during our first year of secondary
school. Many things in our lives had changed. There now
had to be a proper distance between us and the boys we had
grown up with. It was no longer appropriate for us to laugh
audibly in the street or write on the walls. Nadia and I would
pass by the houses of the neighbours who had emigrated,
and when we saw the dry leaves of the trees in their gardens,
we would feel pain. We would both wish to turn into large
clouds to drop a clean rain that would wash the dust off those
leaves.

Sometimes, a deep desire would impel me to go up to
Umm Salli's house and knock on the door. I knew they had
not returned, but I liked knocking. It was the one thing I
could do in order to remember them and feel like they had
not disappeared from our lives. I would look into the garage
alongside the house, and imagine footsteps in the hallway. I
would hear their voices, frozen in the walls. I would feel joy,
seeing their smiles stuck to the windows. I would see tyre
tracks from their car imprinted on the pavement, and hear
the rattle of the engine as it coughed out white exhaust and
hummed to life.

Once when I was little and my father was away from
home, I stood on the stairs with blood flowing from my
nose. My mother picked me up and hurried off with me to
the government clinic in the next neighbourhood. Abu Salli
came out of their house and saw her crying. He quickly went

inside, started his car, and set off after us to take us to the doctor. How I wish at this moment that my nose might be hurt again! I want Abu Salli to carry me in his arms to the doctor. How I have longed for them! For Umm Salli, too, and for their daughters: Salli, Sandus, Sawsan, Sahir and Sulaf. I have longed for my nose to bleed again.

Just like I have told you, I like it when people take care of me, even if it means my nose is hurt and pouring with blood.

My tears fell at their gate, and we continued on our way in silence. In moments when I am sad, I do not like to talk to anyone. Nadia knows this and does not get upset with me.

My silence did not last long. Mala'ika – or 'the Devil', as we used to call her in the shelter back in 1991 – appeared. Without any warning, she came up to us and said, 'I've left school.'

'Why?' Nadia and I asked in shocked unison.

'I've dropped out, and this is my last day. I'm going to burn my books and my notebooks in the bread oven. My mother got divorced yesterday. Father kicked her out of the house. My little sister and I will stay with him.'

'Why don't you and your sister go with your mum?' Nadia asked her.

'My mother is evil,' she replied with a deep sigh. She started to cry.

'Why would you say that about your mother?'

'Because my poor father is a good man, and he does not know the truth about her.' She continued to cry.

Nadia and I stood there, astonished at what she was saying. The Devil looked at us, as though getting ready to say something she had planned out in her head: 'I know the two of you have hated me since the first hour I saw you in the shelter. You are happy that my mother cheated on my father with a stranger. But I hate you too.'

Then she walked away. She called back in a loud voice: 'I'm the Devil, aren't I? I hate everyone in the neighbourhood. All of you are devils!'

8

One winter day – I don't remember exactly which month or year it happened, but most likely around the middle of secondary school – a thick fog spread over our neighbourhood in the morning after a night of intense rain. It was as though a clean shawl were blocking our vision. Tired houses and trees, unseen, were restored to health, and the sparrows moved through the fog like little dots of ink.

Ahmad appeared and stopped his bicycle in front of us at the end of the street. When we came up to him after a few steps, he did not say good morning. He was embarrassed, and it looked like he had not slept. He approached Nadia and put in her hands a piece of paper that had been folded with care. He turned his bicycle around in the opposite direction and shot off, disappearing into the fog.

Nadia was not expecting this surprise. Or maybe she was expecting it, and I did not know.

She opened the paper and began smelling the cologne on it. She read it in a whisper to herself. Then she turned to me and said, 'Ahmad is crazy!'

'Why is he crazy?'

'He says he has loved me since we were in primary school.'

As the day went on, Nadia increasingly lost her sense of the world's heaviness around us. She would get distracted and not pay attention to what I was saying, even when I was talking about something important.

This was the first time that Nadia seemed to let our childhood disappear behind a thick wall of fog. She changed a lot that day. It was as though she were a different Nadia whom I did not know. I wanted to go inside her heart and experience love. But we are not able to use other people's hearts in order to love.

*

Nadia read Ahmad's letter several times as we walked along. She brought it close to her nose to smell it. More than once she made as though to tear it up, but each time she changed her mind at the last moment.

At home, when we returned from school but before she changed her clothes or had lunch with her family, she stood in front of the tall mirror in her mother's bedroom and secretly ran her hands over her body when no one was looking.

Nadia went out to the garden by herself and sat in the delicious winter sunshine, smiling. A delicate breeze blew over her and rustled the leaves, shaking free a few drops of rain that had been clinging to them since the night before. Nadia got up and picked a red damask rose. She scattered its petals in the air, imagining Ahmad's childlike face with his pale eyes, his pointed nose. She inhaled the cologne he had left on his letter, and her spirits soared. Her breast was filled with a gentle, refreshing air. She went inside and stood in front of the mirror a second time, still smiling.

During this time, Nadia began to be afraid of her body. She was afraid of this early discovery of her femininity. She told herself that her eyebrows were beautiful – indeed, none more beautiful had ever graced this world. Her long eyelashes made the colour of her eyes a magical fairy tale. She confirmed that her cheeks were rosy, and her lips attractive. Nadia lifted a strand of hair from her forehead and then softly let it hang down again. She took a small step away from the mirror and pulled her shirt tight around her waist before quickly letting it go again, as though she had done something forbidden.

That night, Nadia sat down to write a long letter to Ahmad. This was the first time she had written a letter. Even in English, when the teacher would ask the class to write a letter to a fictitious friend living in a foreign country, Nadia did not like doing so. Instead of letters, Nadia would choose to write about an imaginary journey to London.

Nadia laid out Ahmad's letter in front of her and began copying its phrases. She wrote, 'I love you,' but scribbled it out. She tried to remember song lyrics and lines from television shows, but she could not remember anything appropriate that matched what she wanted to say. Exactly what did she want to say? She wanted to tell him, 'I love you,' but not to say it directly. In the end, after she began to feel sleepy, she wrote: 'I was delighted to receive your letter, and I liked how you scented it. Before I fell asleep, I thought of you, and when I wake up in the morning, I will think of you again. You have made me think about you.' Then she drew a heart with an arrow and went to sleep.

*

In their first passing encounter the following day, Nadia threw the letter to Ahmad abruptly and then ran towards me, laughing brightly.

She pulled me behind a newspaper stand so we could watch Ahmad from afar as he opened the letter and read it. She was gripping my hand and jumping with happiness as he put it in his bag. He took a few steps forward, and then he stopped and took the letter back out of his bag to read it a second time. Nadia pulled me along by the hand she was squeezing, and we ran off to school.

In geography class, I glanced at her sitting beside me at our desk. She had hidden Ahmad's letter between the pages of the book and was rereading it. She was engrossed, as though she had discovered a new world of words she had never known before.

I glanced at her swiftly in order to confirm that she was still the same friend I loved. This was the first time another person had entered her life, and I was afraid love would steal her from me, that Ahmad would take my place in her heart and share her dreams with her.

During break, I put my hand in hers, and we walked round the courtyard. She was busy looking off into space and paid no attention to me. This boy had taken possession of her spirit and was driving me far away from her. He had filled her thoughts entirely.

Had Ahmad become everything in her life?

'Nadia, I would die for you.'

'And I'd die for you,' she said with a certain coldness, or so I imagined it. I had not expected this reply from her, and I wished she had said something different, something like, 'Why would you say such a thing?'

She opened the letter, still tucked inside the book, and turned her back to me to read it, this time in a whisper. Nadia's innermost thoughts were taking her off by herself, and she was now establishing a private world, far away from me. Her heart throbbed to its own rhythm, and her lungs were breathing air that was not the same air we used to breathe together.

When love proposes its secret history, it begins to guard a sense of uncertainty. It uproots a person from himself, from his family, from his friends, from everything around him, and it holds him in a state of anxiety. Perhaps my existence beside her had faded. She had fallen out of step with me.

One moment she was racing ahead, and another she was behind me. And as our stride fell out of harmony, we began to stumble frequently on our path. It was as though that famous song about love was written just for her:

Confused, eyes now awake to passion
Your pupils blear staying up all night
Plunge down the path ahead
The first step now clear: let's find what comes next!

That year at the beginning of spring, when we went outside at the end of the school day, the downpour we had heard pounding against the windowpanes a short time before had increased. Ahmad was waiting for us at the end of the wall, wearing jeans and a white shirt, with a short leather jacket over the top. Like a passionate hero in the love stories we saw on television, he approached Nadia to hand her a black umbrella before disappearing into the crowd.

'Ahmad is afraid for me – even of the rain!'

In her happiness, she forgot to open the umbrella. She lifted it up, still folded, and waved it in the air, as though telling the rain, 'I love you!'

Nadia actually did love the rain, and she was happy whenever she looked in the sky and saw clouds gathering above her. She anticipated rain before a downpour, and on many sunny days, she told me, 'It's going to rain tomorrow.' And indeed, the clouds in the sky above our school would burst with rain on the following day. It went beyond that. She had a strange affinity with the natural world and its cycles. She watched birds in the sky and knew the times of their migrations; she knew when the seagulls would disappear. 'They are playing over the surface of the river,' she would say. She knew the mating season of the sparrows, and she determined the precise dates on which the flowers would open in the gardens. She spent a lot of time following the lives of insects on the leaves of trees, and when the middle of March arrived, she would say, 'The butterflies are coming,' and so it would be.

She said goodbye to me at the door of her house, and I continued on my way. A few moments later, I heard her footsteps as she panted to catch up. I turned around, and in a voice distorted by a foolish smile, she asked, 'Where do I put the umbrella?'

'Give it to me.' I took it from her and went inside.

If any of you wants to know why I took the umbrella, the matter is very simple and does not require much thought. Nadia would not have had any reply if her mother had asked her, 'Where did you get this umbrella?', whereas I could tell my mother in such a case, 'I got it from Nadia.'

9

As I told you before, we never forgot Baji Nadira. But one day the rain fell and washed her off the wall where we had drawn her sitting beside Uncle Shawkat on a sofa, with a sparrow flying above them. When I passed by this wall, I cried a lot. I cried because I saw Uncle Shawkat sitting by himself while a sparrow, trapped in chalk, flapped its wings above his head. I did not feel pain on account of Baji herself. I felt pain for something else, maybe loneliness.

After Baji Nadira disappeared from his life, Uncle Shawkat did not forget her. Maybe he did not try to. Maybe he had not even considered it. But he did learn to live alone without minding much because he had had grown used to it.

'He's afraid of dying alone,' said my mother as she spoke about him to my father. She went on, 'It's hard for a person to die alone, like a stranger.'

My father was silent as he reflected, not wanting to continue the conversation with her. My mother always makes things more complicated, for in her mind, as I've said, everything is connected to death.

Believe me, I did not understand that. I do not understand why it is hard for a person to die alone. On the contrary, the way I see it, it is hard for a person to live alone because when they die, a person does not need friends.

Every Friday, Uncle Shawkat would get up late. Sometimes he would wake at nine in the morning, and sometimes it would be eleven. Ever since the rain had washed away the picture of his wife that we had drawn on his house, he had been alone. He ate his breakfast alone. He stretched out on the sofa and watched television alone. After a few minutes he would turn it off again, and he was still alone. He did not like to watch the programmes that Baji used to like. His life had changed since she left. He no longer looked at the photo of them under the Geli Ali Beg waterfall, hanging on the wall of the living room, even when he dusted it. The last time he had looked at this picture, he found he was alone.

Uncle Shawkat began sitting alone at the bottom of the stairs in his house to shine his shoes. Then he would get up to gather his clothes from the clothes line and iron them. He would arrange them in his dresser after choosing his clothes for the following workday. Among his clothes was a pink shawl that had belonged to Baji Nadira, which he found in the wash after she had left. Every time he washed his clothes, he put this shawl in with them. He would spread it out on the clothes line with his other things. Then he would iron it and set about putting it carefully away before putting it back in the wash.

After he had done all of that, he would go out to inspect the back garden. He would feed the nightingale and the two partridges. He had noticed in recent days that the nightingale was singing less, and the partridges had become skinny. He began talking to them as he fed them. Then he pretended to ignore them, feeling a painful lump in his chest. He could not do anything for these birds. He knew in the depths of his heart that they were longing for Baji Nadira.

Uncle Shawkat left his lunch on the stove and went out to the street to inspect a neighbour's house that had been abandoned by its family. Ever since the families had left, he had assigned himself the responsibility of preserving these houses, something he never grew tired of. He would go inside, and in that air he would inhale all the years he had breathed with his neighbours, whom he loved and who had become his extended family. Indeed, the neighbours' houses were the storehouse of his memories. When he took care of these houses, he wanted to tell each family member who had lived under its roof, 'I love you. I miss you.' He missed the grown-ups and the children in equal measure.

With one hand, he would push in front of him a lawnmower with its annoying rattle. In his other hand he carried a toolbox.

One day, he decided to look after Umm Ali's house. He took a key ring out of the toolbox, chose one, and opened the padlock on the iron chain. He went through the gate. After cutting the grass, pruning the withered leaves, and running the water in the irrigation canal, he opened the door to the house and went into the front room before wandering through the other rooms and passages.

In the kitchen, he stumbled unexpectedly upon a black dog. It was stretched out on the floor, exhausted and unable to move from severe hunger and thirst. Before he could ask himself where this dog had come from and how it had slipped inside the house when all the doors and windows were locked, he brought a small dish of water to set in front of it. He went quickly back to his own house, took some pieces of meat and some bones from his refrigerator, and returned to give them to the dog, who began eating voraciously.

'How did you get in here?'

The dog looked into his eyes with a glance that implored his kindness, as if to say, 'I don't know.'

'You would have died alone if I hadn't come in here by chance.'

'I'm not afraid to die alone.'

Uncle Shawkat went over and patted the dog's back. Then he carried him gently to his house, put him down in a small tub, and began cleaning his body with soap as he sang a sad song. He dried the dog in the garden sunshine and began caressing its body tenderly as the dog gradually regained its strength. The dog's eyes shone as it rolled joyfully on the grass.

From that day, Uncle Shawkat was never seen in the street without this dog, which he loved and grew accustomed to. The dog at his heels became part of his outward appearance as he walked down the street. It would stop when he did, and it would sit on its haunches whenever Uncle Shawkat became engrossed in conversation with one of the neighbours.

One of the children came and wiped off the bird I had drawn on the wall, and in its place, he used coloured chalk to draw a small dog underneath the sofa that Uncle Shawkat was sitting on. The dog was looking at Uncle Shawkat, who was laughing. (The difference between a smile and a laugh is that the mouth is closed for the former and open for the latter.)

My mother said to my father, 'He has finally come across a companion. He now has a little dog, and he won't die alone after all.'

'What will the dog do when the man dies? Will he go out to tell the people that he is dead?'

'No... You don't understand me. By nature, a person is afraid of dying alone, and when Uncle Shawkat dies, the dog will be there close by him and will watch his soul as it goes up to the sky.'

'And if the dog dies before him?'

'That won't happen.'

The black dog that Uncle Shawkat had stumbled upon in Umm Ali's house was the kind that could communicate through the language of gestures, just as though that were its native language. Uncle Shawkat took advantage of this natural disposition and became skilled at communicating with Biryad. This was the name he gave the dog, using as a good omen the name of a pet dog that had lived in his grandfather's house in the Turkoman quarter of Kirkuk half a century before.

Little Biryad became just another member of the neighbourhood. Everyone liked him and called out to him as they walked past. He knew each native of the neighbourhood individually and never barked at them the way he would at strangers. He would run playfully behind the children as they sped past on their bicycles. He would jump with the girls playing games on the pavement. He would greet the fathers joyfully when they came home from work.

The truly remarkable thing was that the neighbourhood cats, born on the roofs and in the back gardens, were not afraid of Biryad. They would not keep their distance when he unintentionally crossed their path. Even more remarkable was that some of these cats formed a close relationship with him, one that went beyond merely wandering around freely with him at night. We even began to wonder whether Biryad was a cat in a dog's body, or whether the cats had acquired the temperament of puppies.

One of Biryad's characteristics was that he knew all of them. I would see him cut back on his own food in order to share it with the white cats, and he always left them some bones, even if he was still hungry himself. Another one of his peculiarities that I hope you will not find preposterous is that he could predict things before they occurred. If he left Uncle Shawkat's house in the morning and lifted his leg to urinate on the gate of one of the neighbours, that meant only one thing: these neighbours were getting ready to emigrate soon. Thus, by watching whether he urinated on this gate or that, we came to know who would be the next neighbour to make the decision to set off, never to return.

On top of that, Biryad drew numerous inferences about the future. Some of these were a secret between him and Uncle Shawkat, and some he conveyed of his own accord to the sons and daughters of the neighbourhood. For instance, if he hurried up to a young woman and tried to lick her heels, that meant that she would soon get married to the young man of her dreams and live with him happily ever after. That happened often. Hind married Haidar after a courtship of two years. Maha married Hudhayfa, and Manal married Muhammad after Biryad gave each of them the well-known sign.

If Biryad set about biting the book bag of someone as they walked to school, that meant the student was outstanding in their studies and that success was waiting for them in the end. And if he looked for a long time into the face of some old woman, that meant without the slightest doubt that her final hour was drawing near.

10

The sight of Marwa as she held the rifle and shot into the air was irritating on a personal level. I cannot say if I liked it, or if it just annoyed me. Were it not for the way she spun her rifle through the air in front of my face to frighten me, I would not have given the matter a second thought. This happened every Thursday during the flag-raising ceremony at our school.

One day, Marwa was happy and proud to an unbelievable degree when, after firing into the air, she stood in the courtyard with a group of girls to explain the strength of the rifle's recoil. After making sure that everyone understood what a recoil was, she added with vanity and something of a false naivety, 'There's no need to be afraid of it. The whole thing is very simple. I'm strong, and I can control the rifle. The head teacher of the school knows it – see how pleased with me she is every time I fire the rifle during the flag raising.'

I did not understand why we had to fire a rifle every Thursday at the flagpole. Or why the flag always had to be accompanied by the sound of bullets. Our country's flag had a relationship with bullets I did not understand. Bullets were fired for the sake of raising the flag, and when someone was hit in the head with a bullet, the flag was lowered and wrapped around his body. Without the flag, the dead would not be martyrs, and when we draw the flag on the map of the homeland, that means the homeland is a martyr.

Marwa was a clever student. No one denied that. More than once they singled her out as an example for the class.

In addition to that, she was a beautiful and alluring young woman with her prominent breasts, toned and curvy bottom and a long, elegant neck. In truth, she was one of the most beautiful girls in our school. She was cheerful and funny, and she had a remarkable ability to think up pranks. All the teenage boys in the neighbourhood liked her. They would block her path in the street, but she laughed at them and they would stand aside. There were many occasions when boys would take advantage of some situation to intentionally brush against her body. I do not know what to call the feeling that afflicted them all.

Marwa was happy about the effect she had on the boys, but the boy she liked was Ahmad, and no one else. When she ran into him one time as he was walking in the street with Nadia, she became jealous of Nadia and told her friends, 'Come on, let's follow them and sing to embarrass them.'

My love for you's so crazy, my eyes for you so hazy…

Ahmad turned and was about to make some crass remark, but he changed his mind and settled for a dismissive gesture of the hand. Marwa and her friends paid him no attention and kept singing at the top of their voices.

In order to get out of this predicament, Ahmad was forced to say a quick goodbye to Nadia and go the other way. Afterwards, he began to dislike Marwa, and when he happened to see her in the street, he would turn his face away. Nadia no longer liked Marwa either, and she would change direction if they ever crossed paths.

Personally, I liked Marwa. Or at least, I did not hate her. I did not walk the other way when I ran into her. But I liked Nadia more and took her side. When I was with her and we met Marwa and her clique, I would sing in an almost audible voice:

Stand up and greet him; ignore the people's blame
Stand up, stand up against them; let them stomp in rage

Marwa began to hate us. She hated Nadia and Ahmad. She hated me too. And in order to take revenge on us, she went to the deputy head teacher at school and told her that Nadia had an improper relationship with a boy from our neighbourhood named Ahmad. The deputy head called Nadia's mother into the office the following day. She did not, however, tell her, 'Your daughter is in love with someone.' The deputy head was capable of handling this complicated situation. She just advised Nadia's mother to pay attention to her daughter's behaviour at this stage of her life.

To escape Marwa's observations and pestering, Nadia began meeting Ahmad in back streets in the opposite direction from the ones we normally took every day when going home. We could always wind our way along alternative routes to avoid bumping into annoying people. It is true that Marwa was sometimes annoying, but she was not evil. She bothered Ahmad because she loved him, and she persecuted Nadia because Ahmad loved her. It is always easy for us to make it hard for the people we love. Even when we want to tell them we love them, we sometimes say it in a way that upsets them. I am the only person in this world who does not annoy the people she loves. I do not annoy the people I do not love either.

One day, I got a surprise. I was approaching Abu Nabil's shop to buy something when Farouq came up and stopped in front of me, face to face. 'I like you,' he said.

When I hesitated, shocked at this surprise announcement, and couldn't think of anything to say, he gathered his courage and added, 'I love you.'

I remained silent, still not knowing what to say. I forgot why I had come to the shop in the first place. I tried to remember, but I was trembling, and I nearly started crying. I ran home without buying anything and without saying a word to Farouq.

That event was truly unexpected. I washed my face and stood in front of the mirror. I pinched my right cheek to make it pink, and indeed, a small red spot appeared and then disappeared again. For the first time in my life, I stepped away from the mirror so I could see my whole body in it, feeling a sense of shame as I did so. After glancing both ways to make sure that neither of my parents was watching me, I wet my hair with a little water and combed it with my hands. I gave myself a fleeting glance in the mirror and left the house without a second thought. From a distance, I saw Farouq and smiled at him. He tried to come over to say something, but I left him and went back inside without closing the door. In that moment I was afraid and felt that everyone was watching me from their windows or from rooftop balconies.

A few days before that incident – when he told me he loved me, I mean – Farouq had stood at the door of his house as I was in our garden cutting some bunches of grapes that were still sour. He came over and asked for some of these unripe grapes, saying he liked how they tasted. When I cut a bunch and put it in his outstretched hand, my fingers brushed against his. He gave me a smile I did not understand. After he went inside, I thought about it a little and then put it out of my mind.

I was not able to fall asleep easily that night. I tossed and turned in bed as I tried to drive this thought from my mind. But to tell you the truth, I was happy inside. I kept imagining Farouq standing in front of me, repeating, 'I love you ... I love you,' until I fell asleep.

Farouq did not have brothers and sisters. His father worked as a university professor in Libya. There, he got married to a Tunisian woman – not a very beautiful one, according to

Umm Farouq – and lived with her, writing short letters to his wife and son. In the letters, he said that he was doing well, and that he hoped the two of them were also well. He sent them some dollars at the beginning of each month. Farouq was very clever at school, but he was crazy about football and went to the club to practise every day until, later on, he became a famous player.

I do not know why he chose me of all people and told me he loved me. I had never spoken with him, nor had I taken any interest in him. I actually did not think about love at all. I had been enjoying the story of Nadia and Ahmad, and that was enough for me.

Letters from the Mountains

Letters from the Unknown

11

In those days, many soothsayers began passing through our neighbourhood, claiming to know all manner of things. Biryad would follow them and bark in an attempt to prevent them from coming down our street. When their persistence had exhausted his patience, he bit the leg of a fat woman who said she could read fortunes. After that incident, it became very rare for one of those people claiming knowledge of everything to pass our way.

Biryad lost some of his admirers on account of his surprising behaviour. He was no longer loved as much as before because most of the women in our street were superstitious and encouraged anything that they thought might bring them good luck. Even though most of them were educated and had degrees in medicine, chemistry, law and history, they were curious about the future and the world of the unknown. It was not easy for Biryad to deter the visitors because of the women in our neighbourhood.

One day, a tall, thin man with a well-trimmed beard came down our street. He was elegantly dressed in a three-piece suit with the chain of an old watch hanging down from his jacket pocket. The watch itself was in a small pocket on the left side. He told us he could read fortunes, but that he would not offer any help related to summoning good luck. The man was a little suspicious and definitely peculiar. He spoke with a voice that seemed to come directly out of his chest. From time to time, he would pause to pass his right hand over his forehead and then continue speaking where he had left off.

Without a single mistake, this slender man could recite the names of the members of any family when the name of just one of them was mentioned to him. Then he would state their birthdates, one by one, or the father's occupation, along with a description of him and his habits. He even knew on which side a man slept at night.

These were not the only things that made the people trust him and respect him. Biryad's unusual behaviour towards him, which was different from how he treated other strangers, was what made the women feel so comfortable with him. When Biryad saw this man for the first time, he approached calmly to sniff at his heels as he walked. Biryad looked up at his face as though he had known him a long time, and then he went away without barking. When the women saw that, they wondered at first, but they were grateful to Biryad for not driving him off.

To get things started, Umm Manaf – who always stood at her door, watching people – plucked up her courage and went over to the strange man and, without any embarrassment, began to speak to him in the middle of the street. This, of course – speaking to unknown men, I mean – was not considered acceptable behaviour in our neighbourhood, but Umm Manaf wanted to test him and discover for herself his hidden truth, to confirm whether he was a liar or whether his words were true.

The soothsayer gave her a scornful glance and told her, 'This is the first time I've allowed anyone to test me. And also the last.'

He brought his mouth to her ear and spoke about especially personal and private matters related to her married life. Umm Manaf gasped, and her soul nearly escaped through her mouth at the precision of the things he was telling her, as though he had been watching her life on a movie screen.

After Umm Manaf's audacity, the other women became bold enough to approach this soothsayer. Umm Nawar opened the door of her house and invited him to sit on the swing in her garden. She went into the kitchen to bring him a cup of juice, and when she came back after a few minutes, she found most of the women from her street had entered the garden and surrounded the man, begging him to read their fortunes. Umm Nawar asked them all to calm down, to have a seat on a rug she spread over the grass, and to wait their turns, one after another. The women complied with this request.

The soothsayer raised his head to look into the distance as he grasped Shuruq's palm. Following all the others, she had gone up to him, beseeching him to tell her future. He squeezed her hand, while at the same time he glanced sharply at the other women, making them anxious. He put his right hand to his forehead, and after two minutes of reflection, he addressed them all and said, 'None of you has a future in this place.'

After another expectant silence, in which he nearly exhausted their patience, he produced a deep rattle in his chest and continued to speak. 'Sooner or later, this ship will sink with all of you on board.'

'Ship?'

His sentence had landed on their heads like a thunderbolt as they wondered what ship this soothsayer was talking about. Before any of them dared ask for clarification, he changed his tone of voice and said, 'A person is born into this life not from any desire of their own. He comes out on board whatever ship he happens to be born upon. Small ships dock in the large ocean of this world, and each of them carries a group of people whose destinies are bound together. Some of these ships are as big as a continent, some as big as a country, and some the size of a small neighbourhood. Whenever the ship is big, the relationship between its passengers is not strong. The converse is also true. This neighbourhood of yours is a small ship. When the birds pass through its air, they know they are circling a small ship. You don't know that, for it has remained in place for as long as you've been on it. Consider a nursing infant. When it sleeps on a still, motionless bed, it feels like the edges of this bed are the boundaries of the world. You are the children of this boat, you who have lived on it for decades without it taking you anywhere. Thousands of years ago, people used to live upon the earth without feeling it spin them around like a ship moving through infinite space.'

He fell silent for a while and released Shuruq's hand from his grasp. Then he took hold of it again.

'I want to say something important, and I urge you to pay attention. A person lives in this world with two fates. The first is his personal fate, and the second is his social fate. Do you understand what I mean?'

He waited a while, and when he did not get a response, he continued speaking with his head raised high, as though he were addressing the entire neighbourhood.

'From this moment on, I urge you, from this very moment, think only of your personal fate. Do you understand? Think only of your personal fate. Whoever among you can get off the ship this very hour should disembark at once.

'The ocean you are traversing seems calm, doesn't it? Not at all, ladies and gentlemen! By God, it is not at all calm. Storms rage on the horizon. Most certainly, storms are coming. Whoever wants to put drowning to the test, let them remain. But whoever wants safety, let them flee today. Not tomorrow! Jump into the lifeboats that wait for you, and go far from this place.

'Exile is no laughing matter. I know this well. But the heavens have written this fate for you, and there's no escaping it. You will live as exiles whether you remain here in this neighbourhood or flee to distant cities. Your journey has begun with agony. Prepare yourselves!'

A lament rose among the women, and tears burned their cheeks at this miserable news that fell on their heads all at once.

The soothsayer fell silent for a moment. Then he raised his head to follow a small bird circling the garden. He lowered his voice and addressed them again in a subdued tone.

'Listen to me. Don't waste a single minute. There's no time for crying. This is the hour to get ready for a long voyage away from pain. Don't think – even for a moment – of remaining here. Make haste to flee because the storm is approaching with the speed of a madman.'

As he spoke, he imitated someone reeling as though on the deck of a ship tossed about by the waves. 'Look at me! The waves have begun to hurl me right and left. Do you see?'

He straightened up and began walking calmly around the garden. He plucked a few withered leaves from the orange tree. Then he turned to the women and said, in a whisper: 'I don't wish exile upon you. And I don't like to see you suffering from its terrors. I have no personal interest in whether you stay or you go. I passed through your street by chance, and I decided to tell you the truth. But most of the time, the truth is upsetting. In all honesty, I hesitated to carry out my plan. I'm not able to counsel you to stay, even as I'm pierced with sadness when I call upon you to flee. For in the moment of crisis when the pain of staying equals the pain of leaving, you will remember me and cry, "We're ruined!"

'You will live as exiles, and your tears will know no end. I see you there now, in countries of snow and painful winters. You will warm yourselves with memories. This neighbourhood of yours will become nothing more than a song you weep to remember. I see you on dark, lonely paths as you wander, lost, as exiles do. One of you lifts your head to the sky, and with a heart broken with pain, you cry, "What have we done, O heavens above?" And no answer comes.'

With that, the soothsayer resumed his seat. He again put his hand to his forehead and was silent for two minutes, waiting for their tears to dry.

'Do you know the song about the birds and the sun?'

'You mean the song *O birds above, bring them all my love*?' replied Umm Farouq.

'That's the one. That song will be like your homeland in the coming years. You will sing it a thousand times – no! A million. When you become tired, another song will come. Do you know it? I will tell you: "The Soul a Stranger."'

'This song is the new homeland for all of you. When exile comes timidly among you and then throws you into hopelessness, "The Soul a Stranger" will be the long anthem of sadness. When you forget its words, your homeland will be just an old memory you long for, but you will not think of returning. Remember this too.'

He turned his deep gaze upon Shuruq, whose face went pale as he gripped her hand once more.

'At the end of this month, someone will come to you, asking your family for your hand in marriage.'

Before her features could relax with gladness at this happy news, he resumed staring into her face and added, 'Do not consent. Refuse him immediately.'

'What if he comes back to propose again?'

'Refuse him a second time.'

'But…'

'My daughter, I know he loves you. By God, I know that. And I know that you melt with love for him. I know your entire story. Besides all that, I know that he is a sincere man, a faithful man, and successful in life. He is handsome, power-fully built, and he will put a baby in your womb on the very first night. But that is not the whole story. Refuse him without hesitation.'

'Why?' The word tore from her throat in the hoarse voice of agony.

'The truth is painful. Go ahead and say yes if you don't like my words. What do I care? What do I care if you'd like life as a widow, caring for your orphaned boy who will never once see his father?'

He jerked sharply as he spoke these words. Getting up, he left amid Shuruq's confusion and the women's entreaties that he stay a little longer to tell them more about the unknown that was coming their way.

Without another word, the soothsayer headed towards the door with firm steps. He turned in the direction of the main street, walking quickly, his chest puffed out. Biryad followed him to the end of the alley, bade him a respectful farewell, and came back with his tail in the air, hurrying towards Uncle Shawkat's house and jumping over the wall that bordered the garden.

The women's feet froze in place, and each of them began staring at the others as though unable to believe her ears. The owner of the house asked them to sit back down and began preparing tea. Umm Hussam stood up and cleared her throat. Then, in a voice that resembled her husband's, she said, 'This man is a spy. He has foreign troops and wants to terrify us. Their goal is to empty the country of the middle class.'

'It's true. I agree with you. He looked like Lincoln,' replied one of them who worked as a history teacher.

Umm Nawar brought tea and began chatting with them. Before long, they were talking over each other and no one was able to understand a word that was said. When the Baghdad Clock chimed three in the afternoon, they rose and went their separate ways.

Shuruq had left before them. She sat in her room and went between crying for her bad luck and cursing the lying soothsayer, who may have been sent by one of the other women as part of an accursed plot to separate her from her beloved for the sake of some purpose that God alone knew.

'Otherwise,' she said to herself, 'how do I explain his running away after reading my fortune, mine alone, and not reading the others'?' Addressing her image in the mirror, she said again in an audible voice, 'I'll say yes, even if I'm married to Khalil for one night only!'

12

Previously, I had been living the love story of Nadia and Ahmad, enjoying it like a television series whose events were happening immediately before my eyes. I knew they loved each other, but what did it mean that they loved each other? How did this love happen? Why did their features change when they met? I did not know any of that. I only knew their love from the outside, as the events of a love story that my friend was living, and not from inside the love itself, nor in the midst of the secret feelings that were born in the soul, igniting the mind and making the heart beat faster.

Then Farouq came, calm and quiet. He stood before me, face to face, and said, 'I love you.'

He stole my peace of mind and infused my spirit with anxiety. I began to think about him all the time. I would look for him in the street. Each time I passed by the door of his house, I would turn to look. His name was on the tip of my tongue; his image filled my mind. I felt love like a gentle current of electricity touching my soul. I became obsessed with songs and music. Whereas I had previously been devoted to television, the shows no longer interested me. Not *Adnan and Lena*, not *Sinbad and Yasmina*. I had new heroes: Kathem Al-Saher, Haitham Yousif, Hatem Al-Iraqi, Ismail Al-Farwaji, and Muhannad Mohsen.

You ask me why I love you, why I love you
You ask my torment and madness, my longing

People don't ask the sun why it shares its light
People don't ask the moon why it brings them together at night

I would not ask Farouq why he loved me, nor would I tell him why I loved him. Because people do not know why the sun bestows its light, and love is like the sun. We cannot ask why it makes us fly above the ground. It is not true that he loved me because I cut him a bunch of unripe grapes in the garden and put them in his hand. He loved me for some other reason. He did not know why; nor did I.

But why did he not write me a letter with cologne on it, so that I could send one back scented with perfume? How would I tell him, 'I love you too!'? That was the problem. It was not appropriate for a girl to go up to boy and tell him, 'I love you.' That was something that was neither easy nor proper.

When he said that to me in front of the shop, I hesitated, but I smiled at him later the same day. I gave him a smile with meaning in it. I wanted to tell him, 'I love you.' No, I wanted to tell him, 'I like you.' And when he became confused and hesitated in front of me, I would tell him, 'I love you.'

Did I love him? Why had I not felt this love before he declared his own? Was love sleeping before it woke suddenly in my heart? Or was love itself the thing we loved? Living in a thrilling story, where the identity of the protagonists does not actually matter? Everything disappeared from my life, and only this love remained to occupy my mind.

Before I slept, I opened the window and looked towards his house. His room was half-lit. At that moment, he was writing me a long letter. That is what I told myself as I threw myself onto the bed.

In the morning, my feelings had subsided. All of a sudden, everything had changed. Farouq no longer occupied my mind, and I was thinking about other things. But when I found him waiting for me near the school gate, I became confused again and was afraid I would be at a loss for words a second time. Here he was coming towards me – what was I going to say? I like you, or I love you? Or would nothing like that happen at all?

Here he was, calmly approaching, like someone secretly aiming his penalty kick to take the goalie by surprise. My hands were trembling, my heart was pounding, and before he could say a single word, I told him in a whisper, 'Farouq, I love you,' and ran towards the door of the school. I was happy to have freed myself from the weight of these words. I brought them out of my soul and cast them upon him. At the same time, I was afraid. This was the first time in my life I had a secret of my own, private feelings, something I could not tell Mama and Papa.

A few days after that, we started writing scented letters to each other. We began stealing brief, secret meetings with each other. Our neighbourhood became more beautiful. I breathed the air deeply and smelled the intoxicating fragrance of the gardens. In the evening, I would wait for him at my front door. He would pass by and smile at me, and I at him. Then I would run to the mirror and melt from love.

Are you like me? Do you melt when you fall in love? Why do we melt from love? And who invented this beautiful expression, combining the word 'melt' with the word 'love'? Certainly, the first person who said it melted from love and disappeared from this world. Do you remember the story of Mando, who melted from love for the beautiful young woman Joanna, and became a creek?

Nadia shared in the details of our story, but she was not overly passionate. Every now and then, she would say something that I did not like and did not know how to respond to: 'Your love for Farouq is greater than my love for Ahmad.'

I myself was not sure. Did I actually love him more than she loved Ahmad? How would I know? Can love be measured with a ruler?

I loved him. I also loved Mama and Papa and Nadia and Grandmother, and I do not know which of them I loved most. But I thought about Farouq more than I thought about all of them. Indeed, I thought about him all the time. I asked Nadia the same question to find out her thoughts on the matter.

'Do you love Ahmad or your Mama more?'

Nadia laughed because she did not know how to reply. As I have told you, I did not know the answer either. I took her by the hand, and we went out walking down our street. When we reached Abu Nabil's shop, she stopped in the middle of the road as though she had remembered something important and said, 'Listen. I love my mum, but I don't write her secret letters. And I love my dad, but I don't long for him with every song. When you and I meet, my heart doesn't pound. I only write letters to Ahmad. I listen to songs only for his sake. When I meet him, I want to fly.'

I would have been happy for her to keep going, but I could see in her face that she was waiting for my astonishment. I truly was surprised at her response and playfully told her, 'You're a philosopher, Nadia!'

She looked up and composed her features with a feigned haughtiness. She started telling some kind of joke, but Ahmad passed in front of the store and instantly made her forget what she was going to say.

13

When Uncle Shawkat returned from work and arrived at the gate to his house, he was perplexed to see a group of neighbourhood women leaving Umm Nawar's house together and heading for their own homes, their eyes filled with tears. He stopped in the middle of the street, his heart pounding violently out of fear that a tragedy had befallen someone, given that he was not accustomed to seeing so many women gather in one place at that time of the afternoon.

He tried to understand the situation from Biryad, but the dog was moving around him in circles without looking into his eyes. Left to his own thoughts, he guessed that the women were saying goodbye to yet another family whose hour of emigration had come, or that something terrible – God forbid – had happened.

His heart did not calm down until he knocked on the door. Umm Nawar came out to him, her eyes swollen from crying.

'Hello, Umm Nawar. Are you okay?'

'Hello, Abu No One,' she said, using her nickname for the childless man. 'It's nothing.'

'How can it be nothing when your eyes are red from tears?'

'No, really, it's nothing. This man was reading fortunes and it was too much for me. He says we're all going to drown.'

'We're going to drown? Where in the world would all that water come from?'

He said goodbye and walked sadly home with Biryad in tow. After changing his clothes, he ate lunch and tried to take his usual nap, but he was not able to sleep. He got up, put on a pair of overalls, and went out with Biryad keeping watch like his shadow. He carried his tools in one hand and pushed his lawnmower with the other. Today it was time for Umm Salli's house. He had been passing by it for a while now without going inside to tend its garden.

Uncle Shawkat opened the gate and went into the garage. He set his box of tools down, pushed the lawnmower to the edge of the garden, and began running it back and forth, making a pattern of long stripes. He deeply regretted the growth of thickets and weeds in the irrigation canals, and that some ripe blood oranges had fallen from the tree to the ground.

Uncle Shawkat finished cutting the grass. He left the lawnmower where it was as his small dog played around it. He began uprooting the long stalks growing wild in the canals. He picked up all the dried leaves that had fallen to the ground, and he turned on the garden hose to wash the dust off the trees.

Uncle Shawkat went over and let the water flow into the irrigation canals. Then he went inside the house to examine the water pipes and the electrical wiring. He made sure that the entrances and exits were locked. He tried the doors to reassure himself that they actually were locked tight. He found everything as it should be, but then he decided to check the upper floor of the house, which was not part of his normal routine. He climbed the stairs with tired steps and tested the door of the first room. Finding that it was unlocked, he pushed it open and went inside. The room was entirely empty of furniture. A photo had fallen from the wall and lay face down on the dusty floor. He picked it up and examined it more closely. The picture was of an old family. Abu Salli was there with his wife, sitting on a bench in the middle of the garden. On the mother's lap sat the youngest daughter Sulaf, while the other four daughters stood behind them. A thin man with elegant clothes and a trimmed beard was in the background. Uncle Shawkat had not met him and did not think too much about his presence here.

A tear ran down his cheek and fell to the floor. He took out his handkerchief to dry his eyes and resumed examining the faces of the daughters, one after the other. He was surprised to discover that traces of the watches he would imprint upon their left wrists in the days of their childhood were still visible, pointing to some uncertain time.

He put the photo in the pocket of his overalls and went down the stairs. Feeling tired, he sat on one of the steps and tried to hold back the tears. His mind spontaneously recalled his wife, who had disappeared so far away. He remembered that he had no family now, no small daughters whose wrists he could bite. What he most needed in that moment was for a small, slender girl who looked like Baji Nadira to come out of that photo and tell him, 'Don't cry, Papa!'

That word, papa, rang in his ears. In his entire life, he had never been addressed as Papa. He took the photo out of his pocket again and spoke to it.

'You did well, Abu Salli, when you took your daughters away. The neighbourhood is no longer a suitable place to live. The sanctions and the government have ruined our lives, my friend. Day by day, life becomes harder in this place. Many things have changed since you left. Even this house of yours has become a dwelling for loneliness and pain.'

He raised his head towards the window through which the sunlight spread over the stairs and said, 'Does this dust coming through the windows as a broad beam of sunlight find its way back to you? Are these your heavy spirits, which you left behind in this place, your spirits that forgot to go with you? Every speck of dust contains a memory that wants to stay here, suspended in the air. Here's a dream that has not yet been explained. Here's a song that Sulaf left behind. A laugh that Sundus forgot. This dust is all of you, Abu Salli. This dust is your souls.

'Do you remember when you invited me in for the first time, twenty years ago, and we sat in the garden, getting to know each other? Since that distant evening, we have been brothers: brothers who have shared our joys and sorrows every day. Here I am, making a bench out of a dusty stair in your house, cut off by desolation, with no wife to care for me, and no daughter to tell me, "Don't cry, Papa!"

'I am going to cry, Abu Salli. I am going to cry until the river of my tears dries up. Other neighbours departed after you, and still others will leave. I am here alone. I do not have family to go to. You were my family, my loved ones, and I have lost you. I am afraid, my friend, afraid that I will die alone. Do you know the loneliness of dying alone?'

His eyes let the hot tears flow, and he wiped them with his shirtsleeve. He tried to get up and go home, but he felt utterly exhausted. His heart constricted painfully with a renewed desire to weep.

'Don't worry your mind about your house, my friend. I will take care of it. I will look after your garden like I care for my own home and garden. I will care for all the houses. This is my task, O neighbour of my life. After some time, I will sell this house to strangers and send you the money. Neighbours who aren't you will come. I will not get to know them, nor will I want to, because my life does not permit me new friendships. This life, my dear neighbour, does not permit new friendships. I am on the verge of retirement, and I do not know what I ought to do with all this depressing time.'

Another burning tear fell on the stairs. Uncle Shawkat returned the photo to his pocket and got up to leave.

He closed the inner doors behind him, picked up his things, and went out through the gate. Only in that moment did he realise that Biryad was not with him. He went back and looked in every corner of the garden but could not find him. Uncle Shawkat called with his usual whistle, but the dog had vanished. Going back inside, he unlocked the doors again, went up the stairs, and looked in the room where he had found the photo, but without any luck. He decided that Biryad must have gone home ahead of him. He picked up his things once again, pushed the lawnmower in front of him, and left the abandoned house, wrapping the iron chain around the gate.

At the end of the alley, Biryad was jumping up on the legs of a tall man, as though he were talking to him. Uncle Shawkat rubbed his eyes at this strange sight, and when he was able to focus his eyes again, he could not believe what he saw. The man disappeared in a flash, and the dog came hurrying back towards him to lick his feet.

What he had seen was so strange that Uncle Shawkat did not realise he was walking in the opposite direction from his house. After approaching the wrong door a number of times, he came back to his senses, turned around, and pushed the lawnmower with its tiresome rattling until he got back home. And rather than focusing his doubts on the behaviour of the dog, he began to doubt his own mind.

14

Our neighbourhood had not been the same since the soothsayer's visit. It became somewhat depressed, and its people
were afflicted with misgivings about the future, having lost
hope that any sense of well-being would return to their lives.
The soothsayer was not, in fact, responsible for this dejection.
Like a doctor who informs you that you are sick and must
take a bitter medicine immediately, he had merely told us
that we were unhappy.

In those days, men, women and children would sit in small
circles, occupying this corner or that, reviewing the man's
tidings amongst themselves, with each person explaining it
according to their point of view. They all agreed that everything he had said was correct, but they disagreed about the
nature of the truth in his words.

Some people thought everything would happen exactly
as he said. They even went so far as to assert, 'We are now
living aboard a ship, directly under our feet, that is sinking
in the sea. One day this ship will carry us away, or it will
sink right where we stand.' The other group said he had
exaggerated many things and conflated the real with the
imaginary. Strange, unexplained things began happening,
however, especially in those days. In Abu Manaf's house,
there was a small hole under the tiles, through which salt
water began seeping in. After a few days, this hole became
bigger, and some large, shiny fish came through it. Umm
Marwa said her house was rocking at night, as though it were

a small boat with a wave bottled up underneath that wanted to pass to the other side. Umm Nawar said she saw a small whale appear suddenly in her kitchen and then vanish into thin air. I too saw strange things, but I did not tell anyone about them because people do not believe us when we tell them things that have not already occurred to them. I find it strange when they believe their own feeble minds but do not believe others. When people do not want to believe you, do not tell them the things you know.

Abu Hussam had a different point of view. He believed 'that man' – meaning the soothsayer – was 'just a liar and a meddler. He's working for the interests of foreign countries that want to fill our souls with terror because we defied the sanctions.' Everyone fell silent in the face of this opinion that Abu Hussam expressed with such confidence. It was not in anyone's interest to justify and defend the soothsayer because no one knew anything about him other than what he looked like when he suddenly appeared in the neighbourhood. But deep down, we believed the soothsayer spoke the truth, for indeed, things were becoming more complicated for us day by day, and our life in that place had become very hard. It was difficult to know what the future held in store. Our ship rocked amid the buffeting of fierce waves, and our appointment with departure was only a matter of time.

The best indication of the truth of the soothsayer's predictions was Abu Nabil's shop, which had become empty. Many goods were no longer available. The bare top shelves gathered dust, and were it not for the share of provisions he received from the government to distribute among us on the first day of each month, his shop would have closed long before. Our streets became worn out and filled with potholes. The cars going by looked older and older, their windows broken. Fatigue appeared on fathers' faces. Mothers began making substitutions for everything that was no longer available. My mother took out the old sewing machine that we had completely forgotten about. She cleaned it, put oil into the little holes on its sides, and brought it to the living room. We no longer bought new clothes. It was better to repair old clothes and wear them as though they were new.

The sanctions broke forcefully into our lives and spun our heads right around. The neighbourhood women lost their elegance. Likewise, the men no longer paid any attention to their appearance. Even our school building became somewhat faded as despair overwhelmed the head teacher, the deputy head and the staff. All of them, with the exception of Ms Arwa, became more tense and distracted during the lessons. They often gathered together at the door of one of the classrooms to discuss the sanctions and the possibility of quitting their jobs and leaving the country.

In those days there were many protests and demonstrations. From time to time, the deputy head would come to our classes and ask us to go out into the courtyard. There, along with the other schools, we would be organised into wide columns to head out to the main streets carrying banners that criticised the United Nations, the international community, the Security Council, America, Israel, Great Britain, and even France.

Nadia and I took advantage of these opportunities to see Farouq and Ahmad, whose schools would also go out. We would meet in Al-Zawra Park or in the gardens around the Baghdad Clock. Love always makes its own world far from reality. Birth, death and love – these three do not care about reality.

I put my hand in Farouq's and we sat in the shade of an old tree, on the roots of which lovers had been carving their initials for decades.

'Farouq, I'm going to sing you a new song.'
'You don't have a pretty voice, but somehow I'll bear it.'

I crumble before you, just you
But mute, I hold myself high

Farouq laughed his childish laugh that killed me every time. He was laughing because I closed my eyes and sang in all seriousness, as though up on stage in front of a large audience, even though my voice was not at all up to the song. I knew it, but I still wanted to sing in spite of Farouq.

He moved deliberately closer and stretched out his fingers, seeking my own. I kept my hand away, pretending to be preoccupied as I sang the song again. He tried a second time without success.

Give up! I do not love you, tho' you rage and sulk
Give up! Don't make me burn when I see you

Farouq laughed again. 'You truly are crazy.'

Farouq, give up! I do love you, love you entirely
Give up! I burn when I see you!

Farouq choked with laughter. I got up and playfully ran away, my plaits dancing in the wind. He followed with the grace of an athlete and ventured to reach out and grab my fingers, which resisted for a few seconds and then gave in, melting in his hand as a fire blazed in my soul. My God, how lovely to intertwine fingers as they make love like blind white cats born in the cold.

'Farouq, let go. It's killing me!'

He stopped in the middle of the road and burst out laughing.

'Don't be afraid – you're not going to die!'

'No, let go! That's enough – don't be greedy.'

Farouq did not let go of my fingers, and my fingers did not want him to. I did not know what I wanted. When some diabolical influence brushed his fingertips against mine, light flooded my veins. When he looked at my lips, I knew exactly what he wanted, and I turned my face away. In those few seconds, when I turned my face away to escape his meaningful look, my head spun with the kind of dizziness I loved. I felt my head get light, and I forgot the world. In those moments, I forgot the world entirely, and this forgetting is the sole blessing of love. I looked into his eyes again, and I knew in that instant that he forgot the world too. In our whole lives, we experience only a few seconds in which we forget like that. How can I explain it to you? The one thing I can tell you is that love works against memory. I do not know how that happens, nor why. I just love this dizziness that lasts for a few seconds while I forget the world.

The next day, a pupil from a different year – her name was Shams, as best I can remember – knocked on the door of our class and handed a piece of paper to the teacher. The teacher read out my name and Nadia's and said, 'The deputy head wants to see you in her office.'

Mrs Athmar appeared angrier than usual this time. She spoke with fire and brimstone as she rebuked us for having left the procession. But at the same time, she was a good-hearted woman, and her anger quickly subsided. After her outburst quietened into a kind of reproach, she said, 'This is the last time.'

'Yes, ma'am.'

We went out of her room, laughing with joy. In love, there is no last time, Mrs Athmar! Nadia and I do not grow tired of love; we melt from love, Mrs Athmar!

Marwa too: she did not grow tired of telling on people, and whenever she brought Mrs Athmar the names of pupils who had left the procession to sneak out the back, Nadia and I were at the top of the list. Mrs Athmar did not like Marwa. One day, she became fed up and told her, 'After today, I don't want any news about other pupils. Everything that happens outside school is not the school's affair.' She ordered Marwa to leave and slammed the door behind her.

That same evening, Marwa went to Nadia's home and told her brother Muayad, 'Your sister left class to go out with Ahmad.'

Muayad became angry and informed his mother and father immediately. He went up to Nadia's room and searched her books and notebooks. He began watching her as she left school, and it became hard for her to leave home in the afternoon and wander around the street as we always used to do.

During this time, Nadia began loving Ahmad more than ever. She began to long for him every moment. She dreamed of running away with him to some distant country, like Adnan and Lena, who ran away to the Isle of Safety. She filled her notebooks with ideas about separation, love, sleepless nights and desire. She drew candles dripping wax in a dark night. She closed her eyes and sent her soul into his arms. She wanted him to come in through her window and suddenly take her in his arms and kiss her. He would whisper, 'I love you,' a thousand times in her ears and say, 'Nadia, I die in your eyes.' But Nadia was besieged by her mother and her brother. In the evenings, Muhannad Mohsen appeared

on the television screen. He looked straight at Nadia and
sang for her:

> *Their fear for you so great*
> *Their guard, he keeps me apart*

One day, we left school for a new procession. That was the
day of the big tour that the British parliamentarian George
Galloway made through the streets of Baghdad. It included
a review of the 'Children of Iraq against the Sanctions'.
Standing in the main street, we waited for Galloway's red
double-decker bus. We raised old photos of the president
and sang patriotic anthems together with the school head
teacher. At the same time, we were thinking of a way to slip
away without anyone noticing.

A little before the procession arrived, Nadia and I secretly
moved into the back row of students and took a few steps
back. When the procession had arrived directly in front of us
and everyone surged forward, we hurried towards the fence
of Al-Zawra Park, walking along it until we entered the gate
and disappeared among the trees. The gate of Al-Zawra
marked the moment you entered forgetfulness. It was a deep
passage into ourselves, far away from politics. Politics took
people away, stealing them from themselves and blending
their feelings with those of others until a person no longer
even knew their true self.

One time, when we passed near the gate of Al-Zawra,
we found it closed with a sign that read, 'The park is closed
for renovation.' The Al-Zawra had driven us out of its
walls and into the world of politics and slogans. The world
became narrow, and I felt stifled. The existence of gates like
Al-Zawra's was a kind of hope. Do you know what I mean?
In order to make myself sufficiently clear, let me say that love

needs merciful places too. It chokes when the air is filled with slogans.

'Down with the tyrannical sanctions!' Nadia shouted as she ran longingly towards Ahmad, who had arrived before us with Farouq. Nadia used the international blockade to break her familial blockade. Blockades came in different forms, and one drove out another. Nadia put her hand in Ahmad's, and the two disappeared among the thick trees.

I crumble before you, just you
But mute, I hold myself high

Farouq and I sat in the shade of a tree. In an embarrassed voice, I sang him a song by Haitham Yousif while my hands planted themselves in his.

I turned around to look back. There, in the shade of a giant eucalyptus tree, Nadia and Ahmad were forgetting the world and creating another moment for love. From that distance, I saw her smile, and my heart was at ease.

I lived my whole life looking back, watching from a distance for her smile to put my heart at ease.

15

In a state of shock at the soothsayer's words, Shuruq did not sleep the night after she left Umm Nawar's house. She turned over in her head what he had said twenty times, though not for the sake of finding the answer, for she had decided the matter within herself and no longer debated the idea of marrying Khalil. The question was settled as far as she was concerned.

What occupied her and caused all this anxiety now was what the future held after the wedding.

'Say yes if you'd like life as a widow, caring for an orphaned boy who will never once see his father.'

She touched her stomach and felt the movement of a foetus. He kicked inside her, and she could almost hear the sound of him crying, even though she had not yet got married let alone become pregnant.

She imagined the wedding night she had long been planning: the long, white dress; her new blonde hair, with small, shiny sequins spread over it. She imagined the small cottage where she would live with Khalil, who would return to her in the afternoon, tired from his back-breaking work in the military manufacturing division. She imagined all the details he had mentioned to her regarding their life together. She sat on her bed and began to cry.

Shuruq had fallen in love with Khalil less than a year before when she met him by chance. At that time, she was still a student in her final year of college. He had preceded her by several years and graduated as an engineer from the University of Technology. After graduation, he had joined one of the secret plants connected with military manufacturing. His elegant appearance, his tall stature, his fit and graceful body and his powerful manliness all attracted her. So did the strength of his muscular arms, sleeves rolled up to his elbows. When he looked at her for the first time, she had stumbled, had forgotten the world, had nearly fallen down in the street. This was the man she had been dreaming of since her first days of puberty.

Her dreams never carried her far in terms of her desires. All she wanted in life was a man like this. A young man with a reasonable level of income, a small house and an old Lada car. She did not know precisely why she had chosen that type of car, but she was unable to imagine any other kind.

Shuruq tried as hard as she could to maintain her composure under the power of his gaze as she walked past. But she could not resist the temptation to turn back, overcome by the urge to steal a fleeting glance at his athletic build and his broad shoulders.

Her turning around coincided with his own as he looked her over. In that moment, all the inaccessibility she had practised in the face of solicitations and flirting from students at the university collapsed, and she smiled at him. She was rooted in place and forgot to keep walking. He came over and asked her name.

'Shuruq.'

'A lovely name!' He looked in her eyes and added, 'Miss Shuruq, keep walking on your way in the opposite direction, and I will follow you. I want to speak with you a little, if you don't mind?'

She changed directions, crossed the street, and waited for him there, thinking about the enchanting way he mispronounced the letter 'r' in her name.

She walked with him that day until evening, forgetting she
had to return home. She nearly melted in front of him. Her
femininity exploded, and her body was burning under her
clothes.

Khalil was not a flirtatious type of man. At that stage of his
life, he was looking to settle down with a suitable wife. And on
that day, he had come across Shuruq. He never thought of
exploiting her obvious moment of weakness before him. He
spoke to her openly about marriage, the future and children.

That day was actually her birthday. Never before in her
life had she felt so happy.

After two or three meetings, he decided to make an official
proposal. He asked her to pick an appropriate time for him
to visit her family. Shuruq's parents, however, did not want
her to think about marriage at all; she had to complete her
final year of studies before she could consider it. Shuruq
lived through a hard year of study. She wanted the days to
go by faster than they did, but time and love are a complicated equation. When we are in love, time moves as fast as a
train. But when waiting for love, the lazy minutes creep by,
dragging themselves along as if on the way to bed for a long
sleep.

Shuruq finally graduated from university, and she and
Khalil had agreed on the following Sunday as a date for their
engagement. That was when the soothsayer appeared and
ruined her happiness.

She touched her belly again. The foetus she imagined
moving inside her made her happy. But she quickly broke
into sobs when she remembered that he would come into this
world without knowing his father.

She felt boxed in by the stuffy air in the room. She put
her mother's abaya over her head and went out to the street
without asking her family's permission as she always did

when going the market or visiting her friends in the neigh-bouring streets.

She walked towards the main street without having decided yet where she would stop. Then she turned and went back. The soothsayer appeared before her in a bus driver's uniform. She hurried up to him and blocked his path in order to speak to him, but he did not recognise her. It seemed as though he found her behaviour odd. He took a step back and asked in surprise, 'What's the matter, miss?

'I want you to tell me the truth!'

'What truth are you talking about, my daughter?'

'Don't try to get away! I know you perfectly. Even your voice is the same.'

Before saying a single word, he put his right hand on his forehead and fell silent for several moments as he contem-plated her face. A red bus stopped beside him. He climbed aboard, and it carried him quickly away. He smiled at her through the window and was gone.

Biryad came and licked her heel. She looked at the dog panting before her as though he were trying to say, 'Come on!'

Biryad walked in front of her. Shuruq followed until he stopped in front of her house. She went inside without closing the door behind her.

16

We saw Ahmad ahead of us, carrying his schoolbooks in one hand, without a book bag. He had a lit cigarette between his fingers, and wisps of smoke rose from his nose to form circles that surged above his head, spreading through the cold air. This was the first time we had seen him smoking.

He walked towards us, and when he had come close, he took a quick drag from his cigarette and threw it on the ground, putting it out with his shoe.

'Nadia, would it be possible for me to see you at the Baghdad Clock?'

Nadia was afraid on account of her family. She did not want to create new problems for herself at home or at school. But she was dying to see Ahmad, and a long time had passed without a meeting. She asked my advice, and without thinking I told her, 'Go!'

'Will you come with me?'

'No.'

'But I'm afraid.'

'Don't be afraid.'

'But it's going to rain in a little while.'

'Nadia, don't be silly. Rain has nothing to do with it.'

Nadia smiled. Nadia, who always used to say she liked the rain, liked clouds, and liked listening to music during a rainfall when we were little. I think it was when we were in our third year at school that she went out one evening with her family for a drive, and it happened that they were caught in a shower during the trip. Later that day, when she got back, she told me, 'The car's windscreen wipers were the most beautiful thing I've seen in my whole life. The radio was playing beautiful music, the most beautiful I've ever heard. Drops of water were collecting on the glass. The wipers moved quickly, gathering the drops together, and the water ran down the sides of the car like a little waterfall. It was the most beautiful thing I've seen in my entire life.'

That was a beautiful thing. Indeed, the most beautiful thing Nadia had seen in her life. Whenever rain fell on our car windows, and the wipers came on, I would see it with Nadia's eyes. There are many things in this world we love through the eyes of others. We love them through the eyes of the people we love. The rain, the windows, the music and the wipers are a perfect example of that kind of thing.

That was the first date between Nadia and Ahmad that took place without me. Farouq was out of the country in Argentina with the youth national team, and my presence with her when she met Ahmad was no longer necessary. She would skip school and meet him. She did not need me to be her alibi with her mother. But the next day, she would use me as a witness before the deputy head to invent a new story explaining where she had been.

'Ma'am, perhaps Nadia has got engaged and is too embarrassed to say.' That was the latest excuse that I used those days. I had given many excuses previously, some of which the deputy head believed, and some of which she did not. But in any case, she would always smile.

The news of Nadia's engagement, which I had invented for the deputy head, spread to the teachers, and from there it passed by some quick means into the mouths of the students and was transformed into a song specifically about Nadia.

Truly, you're engaged, little lady; truly he loves you true.

Baydaa sang in the classroom with her enchanting voice while the other girls kept the beat on their desks with their fingertips. Meanwhile, one of the girls kept watch on the hallway through the half-closed door, even as she drummed on it with her fingers.

Wijdan climbed up on a desk and danced like someone intoxicated. Encouraged by her example, girls jumped onto their chairs in the moment of madness that the rumour created. The sound of drumming rose, hips shook and chaos reigned. An irate Ms Arwa banged on the door of the classroom, and in the briefest moment order was restored. She looked around at our faces, one by one, taking pride in our surprised silence as we sat down, motionless wooden statues. Ms Arwa's lips started to smile, and then she burst into laughter and left. Baydaa resumed singing in a low voice. Wijdan stopped dancing when Nadia herself arrived. When Nadia danced, everyone had to make way for her.

That evening, our youth national team was playing against the Canadian team in Argentina. The streets of our neighbourhood were empty as everyone sat in front of the television. In the twenty-third minute of the match, Farouq scored a goal, driving the ball into the Canadian team's net. In front of the television cameras, he ripped off his shiny black jersey adorned with the Iraqi flag to show a map of Iraq drawn over his heart. The entire neighbourhood emptied into the street. The kids, followed by Biryad, gathered at the door of Umm Farouq's house chanting, 'This is how the besieged play! This is how the besieged play!'

When their national team puts a goal in the opponent's net, we are the only people in this entire world who weep.

17

One of the things about Biryad that never ceased to surprise Uncle Shawkat and the whole neighbourhood was that the colour of his tail was white, unlike the colour of his body, which was black. It made him look quite odd. Our neighbourhood did not have much knowledge of dogs so we did not know whether this happened naturally with other dogs or whether it was specific to this strange dog that had become part of our lives.

'Old age makes inroads on dogs from the tail, and on cats from the ears!' That was something Abu Hussam declared with great certainty to a group of his friends as they sat together for their daily session in front of Abu Nabil's shop. One of the boys overheard this conversation, and he spread its contents to his friends, with several additions of course. Instantly, this theory became established as a firm scientific truth that brooked no dissent. To add to our conviction of its accuracy, we began watching the ears of cats to notice any changes that happened to them as they got older. By pure coincidence, the ears of the cats in our neighbourhood did turn white.

That week, with the usual sign that we all knew, Biryad urinated in front of two houses. One of the families emigrated in the middle of the week, and the second family made preparations to do so. The final decision had been made, and all that remained was to carry it out. This discouraging news left traces of sadness on everyone's face. A family's

emigration from the neighbourhood was no less painful than
the amputation of a limb from the body.

Wijdan's family emigrated that week. Widjan left, her
sister Samah left, and so did her sister Tayiba and their
brother Mahab. Their mother, Dr Safaa left, as did their
father.

The gate of their house was locked with an iron chain,
and the keys were entrusted to Uncle Shawkat, along with a
long letter that contained a message of farewell to the entire
neighbourhood.

In the midst of this sorrowful atmosphere, the soothsayer
appeared in the street a second time. He had got rid of his
beard entirely and wore a pair of dark glasses, the kind that
blind people sometimes wear. He had altered his appearance
in other ways too. One addition was a long cane he carried,
not leaning upon it but rather waving it about in the air.
He had an old book with a dog-eared cover under his arm.
He walked with confident steps as he whistled 'The Soul a
Stranger'.

News of his appearance spread quickly throughout the
neighbourhood. Biryad went out to welcome him, followed
by some of the women, each of whom invited him into her
home. 'God bless you! Come and visit us!'

But this time, he preferred to go to Umm Mustafa's house
because he knew she would emigrate with her family in a few
days. We all knew that too because Biryad had lifted his leg
and urinated on their gate.

Umm Mustafa brought a chair out into the garden for the
soothsayer. He collapsed into it and stretched his legs out in
front of him, waving his stick in the air. Women gathered
around on all sides. The man cleared his throat. He looked
at Umm Mustafa and thanked her for her hospitality. Then

he said to her coldly, 'I wish a happy trip for you and your family. Your stay in Jordan will be somewhat long, but don't be afraid: after that, everything will be as it should. This is the last time I will see you. Arm yourself with patience, and be strong. Exile is a bitter medicine, but it must be drunk. Its taste will remain in your mouth until the end.'

When Shuruq interrupted him with a sob, he gave her a malicious smile and said, 'Happy future marriage! You've made your choice; it's all over.'

He did not look at her face again, as though to indicate that he had nothing left to say to her. Shuruq understood and left Umm Mustafa's garden immediately, cursing in her heart the hour in which she first saw his face.

The man told the women to calm down and sit in front of him on the grass. He put his right hand to his forehead as if to take his temperature and was silent for a couple minutes as he looked into the women's faces. He opened his book and passed his eyes quickly over some of its pages. Then he closed the book and set it aside. He spoke with a voice that came straight from his chest, saying, 'None of you has any future at all in this place.'

Before any murmuring could break out, one of them – I am not sure which – asked the name of her eldest son. When the man answered, he also mentioned the name of the head of the household, along with the name of his father and grandfather. She opened her mouth in wonder at his remarkable ability to know these personal details even though she had had met him only once before, during the previous occasion in Umm Nawar's house. Another woman asked the same question, and a similar answer came. The women sank into silence as they watched the dignified features of his face. He too fell quiet every time he touched his forehead.

He told Umm Nadia, even before she asked, 'You will emigrate with your family to Syria. Your only son, in turn, will leave you a year after you settle there to emigrate to Australia.' She shook her head incredulously and asked him about Nadia's future. The man gave a soothing smile to reassure her even as he avoided the details.

He told Umm Farouq, 'Your son will soon quit football and get married in a distant country. Your husband will come back to you after he has grown old and useless.'

He informed Umm Baydaa about her emigration and the fate of her daughter. Then he turned to my mother and told her, 'Your daughter will carry the neighbourhood with her wherever she goes, guarding it against oblivion.'

The man felt his forehead and was quiet for two minutes. He focused again on my mother, who was thinking that moment about leaving Umm Mustafa's house. As though he knew her intention, he made a commanding gesture with his cane to bid her stay a little longer. In a dramatic voice, he proclaimed, 'Verily, the future to her shall be revealed!'

He picked up his book and stood, neglecting his cane and using the back of his chair for support. He walked around the garden, and without focusing his gaze on any particular thing, he came to a halt behind the women, who all turned towards him, waiting for news of the unknown. He resumed looking at their faces, one after the other. 'Oh!' The sound emanated suddenly from his chest. He touched his forehead.

'None of you has any future at all in this place,' he repeated. He went on to add, 'A man lives in this world with two fates. The first is his individual fate, and the second is his fate with his compatriots, for a man cannot live alone. But it is first necessary that he live, that he survive, that he exist. Then he will meet those with whom he will live.

'When a ship is about to sink, the passenger on board thinks first about his individual fate, ignoring what happens to the others. Before anything else, he wants to save his own life, and he jumps into the lifeboat at the first opportunity. After reaching shore, he begins looking for the people with whom he will spend his life, but unfortunately, he fails, because he remains bound by the strength of memory to others, to those with whom he has developed a spiritual history. Therefore, he will remain an exile till the end. Do you really know what it means for a person to remain an exile till the end? That he abandons the mother tongue that has established its spiritual history within him. And that he spends the rest of his life contrary to the laws of this spirit. For that reason, exile is always an exile of the soul, an eternal distance between body and soul that rends a man's being and throws him into the storm.'

The soothsayer stopped where he was and began chanting the words of 'The Soul a Stranger'. The trees, the birds and the air all echoed it back to him, and the place was filled with the sound. The melody stole inside everyone present and played upon their spirits. After the song ended, he looked at them with a half-smile on his face.

'I know this neighbourhood is precious to your hearts. The memories in it are precious to your souls. The land whose air fills your lungs is the most valuable in this world. But what will you do when the ship is about to sink? You will spend what remains of your life aboard lifeboats rocked by violent waves in the middle of the oceans. There is no shore nearby to seek refuge, no friendly harbour whose lighthouse shines through your night.

'Even the distant countries that your feet tread upon will treat you as spiritual commodities, piled up in the storehouse of forgetfulness. The night of your tears will grow long. You

will bury your dead in elegant cemeteries where they will lie
under vainglorious flowers.

'The dead... Maybe they are the only happy ones among
you. Every evening, your souls will leave the foreign land to
come here and float through the sky of this neighbourhood.
They will knock on the doors of the houses where they lived
the most beautiful years of their lives. But sadly, strangers
will open these doors to them. The houses in turn will deny
them and forget the spirits that made their mark on the walls.
But the dead have the freedom to live in the times and places
they want. They will gather once again at the shop of Abu
Nabil every night to gossip until their ghosts are content.

'I'm not here to sow despair in your souls. Don't believe,
any one of you, that I am just a harbinger of calamity or
the ill-omened firebird. I'm telling you everything I know.
I'm telling it for your sake and for the sake of your children.
Without any recompense. I don't want even a word of
thanks. These sanctions are long and will not soon end.
When their end does come, war will begin, and then everything will disappear into oblivion.

'Neighbour will deny neighbour, friend will deny friend,
brother will deny brother. People's bodies will be thrown to
the dogs at night. The pavements will be choked with the
dead. Terror will enter your houses through the windows.
You, the middle class, who form the pillars of society, you
have no weapons to defend yourselves. You are the no man's
land of every war, the easy target for all the weapons crossing
above your heads.

'Your neighbourhood will live dry days in air that burns
the face. Death will wander past like storm winds through
an abandoned village. Sunset will give birth to terror that
sleeps in your beds. Strangers will suddenly appear out of the
abandoned houses, talking about you in strange languages.

They will open fire in cold blood, without batting an eye. Bullets will spray in every direction. Innocent bodies will be pierced without crying out. One of you will pass a neighbour's corpse lying in the street, and you'll touch your own body and thank the heavens that it is still breathing. Start breathing distant air before the air here runs out!'

He fell silent for a while, looking at the canal to his left. He pointed his stick at the flowers scattered about without any order, swaying in the breeze.

'There's nothing more melancholy than a morning rose opening in the garden of an abandoned house.'

He turned to pick up his book. Although he did not need to, he leaned on his stick as he straightened up and immediately departed. Biryad followed him to the end of the alley and then hurried back, hanging his head in sadness.

Silence settled on the women for several minutes. They feared the unknown, the hidden parts of the future, the uncertainty of setting off, and the risk of staying.

'Liar.' Umm Farouq spoke the word without being fully convinced of its truth.

Umm Mustafa replied, 'He's not a liar. Your husband will not return before the Tunisian woman drinks up his vigour and sends him to you in the mail like a worn-out scrap of cloth.'

'I don't know,' said Umm Farouq.

My mother said, 'He didn't demand a single dinar in exchange for his words, so how could he be a liar?'

'Let's wait and see,' responded Umm Farouq.

'We'd better not wait too long,' said Umm Baydaa.

The Baghdad Clock struck three in the afternoon. The women got up and headed over to Umm Mustafa to say goodbye, hot tears in their eyes. They pressed her close and departed for home.

18

Biryad entered Nadia's dream and said, 'Follow me.' He lifted his white tail as he led her through the gate of Abu Hussam's house. He went to the place where his daughter Mayada was lying. Nadia looked at her face and saw she was dead. She lifted Mayada's hand off the floor and pressed it to her chest. Mayada turned her head away and closed her eyes. Startled at this movement in death, Nadia took a step back. Then she went forward again, took Mayada's hand, and felt her pulse. Mayada moved her lips and addressed Nadia.

'Sit me up.'

Nadia bent over and helped her into a seated position, leaning her back against an old car tyre that was nearby.

'Who killed you?'

'Hussam. My brother Hussam.'

'Why did he do that?'

'A few days ago, I returned to the clinic of Dr Tawfiq. Do you know him?'

'No,' replied Nadia.

'He's a young doctor who opened his clinic two months ago at the end of the street. My neck was hurting, and I wasn't able to sleep on my right side from the intensity of the pain. So I went to him. After the examination, he looked in my eyes and smiled tenderly at me. Then, very deliberately, he left his home telephone number for me along with a prescription.

'After hesitating a long time, I decided to call him because he was a good young man, and I liked his smile. I lifted the telephone to my ear and put my finger on the number three, the first digit of his number. My breaths came short from embarrassment and confusion. I dialled the rest of the numbers with difficulty. It started to ring, and my heart nearly jumped out of my mouth. Help me sit up straighter,' Mayada said abruptly. ' My back hurts.'

Nadia lifted her and leaned her directly against a wall. 'What happened after that call?' she asked.

'The doctor asked to see me again. An innocent relationship developed between us. I liked him and felt safe with him. He had a good heart, and I liked his smile.

'In those days, I began standing for long periods in front of the mirror that hung on the wall in our entryway. I began looking for my spirit after ignoring it for a long time. I started taking an interest in my hair, which I had also been neglecting. I bought a new box of make-up. We started going out together when he had free time.

'I was happy with him until that terrible day. We went to the nursery near the park, and I picked out some plants and flowerpots that he liked. He told me he was going to build us a small house with a garden, not too big. I was very happy and told him, "It will be the most beautiful garden in the world when our children play in it." He laughed and put his hand on my shoulder. I pulled myself away, nearly dying from embarrassment.

'We put the plants in the trunk of his car and went on a drive together through the park. He got out at the refreshment stand to buy us some ice cream while I remained alone in the car. Hussam drove past in a different car and saw me sitting in Tawfiq's. I fainted from fear because Hussam gets angry quickly and looks for conflict. Tawfiq came back a few minutes later and reassured me. He told me he would come in two days to ask my family for an engagement. I was overjoyed and gave him a kiss on the cheek. It was the first time I had kissed him. Believe me, it was only the first time.

'That evening, Hussam came home furious. He found me singing in the kitchen and told me he wanted to talk to me. But I ignored him since I knew he only wanted to stir up trouble. He came over to grab my dress and pull me around.

'"What were you doing in the doctor's car?"

'"Tawfiq wants to marry me."

'"He was marrying you at the refreshments stand?"

'"He'll come here the day after tomorrow to propose. I will marry him and never see your hateful face again!"

'Hussam was seized by a sudden fit of hysteria. He began screaming like a crazy man as he threw plates and glasses at me. Then he ran to our father's wardrobe, took a pistol out of the drawer, and pointed it at my chest.'

✷

When news of this terrible event spread, the neighbourhood was profoundly shocked. The police came and discovered the crime scene. That day was truly a dark one, leaving behind a deep wound in all our souls.

Everybody in the neighbourhood had loved Mayada, who was known for her good nature and the way she helped others. She would always do housework for mothers after they gave birth, and during exam periods, she would go from house to house to offer free tutoring to the boys and girls. When she was studying at the Agricultural College, and even after graduation, she helped everyone arrange their gardens and offered advice regarding fertiliser, the type of soil, and how much water was required. The credit goes entirely to her that the gardens in our neighbourhood were greener and better maintained than elsewhere.

Her father had been a manager at the railway company and had retired a long time ago. As for her brother Hussam, he was a dubious individual who did not mix with any of the other residents of the neighbourhood. Nor would he greet them. He hated Biryad and kicked him once on the mouth. It was the first time that the beloved dog had been hurt by any of the neighbourhood people. Biryad yelped in pain but did not tell Uncle Shawkat what had happened.

Hussam was always on edge. He repeatedly changed his mind after making decisions. A few years before, he had proposed to Wafaa, the daughter of Umm Ali, but then he broke off the engagement without telling her or her family why. He would sometimes walk around drunk and fall down in the street, and the boys would carry him home. Then, not too long afterwards, he surprised us by becoming very religious and spending his days at various mosques. He would disappear for long periods of time, and when he came back, he would distribute religious books to the neighbours for no apparent reason.

Mayada graduated from college when I was halfway through secondary school. She was appointed to a position in a faraway province, but she refused to take the job, preferring to stay at home. As the years went by she began to lose her beauty and grace, and she developed an air of neglect and despair. When fate smiled upon her and Dr Tawfiq fell in love with her, she was transported out of this world.

The police detained Abu Hussam for several days. Then they released him since the suspect, his son Hussam, had escaped to Jordan and was out of reach. The father resumed his old habit of sitting at Abu Nabil's shop with the retired neighbours. He used to sit with them there for many hours without ever getting bored, telling them exciting stories of his life spent working on trains and all the strange things that had happened. But after the murder of his daughter, he became a man of few words, and no one heard his former decisive declarations that brooked no dissent – with one exception: 'It appears that this soothsayer was right.'

This was the first time Abu Hussam had agreed with the sons of the neighbourhood in their expectations. When he realised that, he fell silent for a while and then changed the topic of conversation.

19

Nadia and I recalled the dream on the way to school. We spoke about Mayada and her family. When we saw Biryad playing in the street, we remembered how Hussam had kicked him in the mouth, and how Biryad had hated him since then and would never go near their house.

Nadia and I mixed dreams with real life, fantasies with reality. But she forgot, and I remembered. That day, Farouq came out of his house wearing athletic shorts. Without closing the door, he came after us, and when we turned in the direction of the small square that separated our street from the school, he caught up with us, and as he continued on his way, he told me, 'I miss you and need to speak with you.'

I said goodbye to Nadia with a quick sign and let her go on alone. I followed Farouq. I missed him too, not having seen him since his trip to Argentina. School could go to hell! I watched Farouq from behind as he went on ahead. I felt that every fibre of his being was returning to me. I loved him, and I hoped he would lift me off the ground in front of everyone and tell me he loved me.

We reached the street that ran behind the market. From there, we headed towards the main street, which we followed in the direction of the Baghdad Clock.

We spent some time sitting in the garden facing the clock. I was somewhat nervous because this was the first time I had skipped school. At the same time, I was feeling sad that Mayada had been killed by her brother. But Farouq had been travelling, I had not seen him for ages, and he did not want anything in this world to ruin his joy at their victory.

I tried to act normal with him, but he could tell that my thoughts were elsewhere, so he took me by the hand and we walked to Al-Zawra Park. On the way, he talked non-stop, describing his trip to Argentina for me. He was telling me, 'In the newspapers, they gave me the nickname "The Iraqi Maradona".'

I did not know who Maradona was, but I guessed that he was the best football player in the world, so I smiled at Farouq, encouraging him to go on. But he started looking at the street, the pavement, the litter in the road, and comparing it with the clean city of Buenos Aires that he liked so much. He said, 'The streets there are very beautiful. The buildings are tall, and they aren't covered in dust like the ones we have here.' He also told me, 'Every time I saw a beautiful Argentinian girl, I thought of you and missed you.'

When we entered Al-Zawra Park, he gradually led me on among the trees. He looked both ways, as though he were planning to do something, and then he quickly came close and stole a fleeting kiss from my lips. Automatically, my hands pushed him away, and I immediately realised my mistake. I tried to pull away from him, but I felt an intense dizziness. I lost my balance and nearly fell into an irrigation canal after dropping my book bag. I hated Farouq and decided to leave him and go back to school. But instead, I sat on the ground, put my hands over my eyes, and started to cry.

Farouq sat down a good distance away. He regretted what he had done, and after a short time, he came over to apologise. I do not know why I wished in that moment he would kiss me again. I grabbed his hand and felt the heat of his fingers. He began wiping my tears with his other hand, but he did not kiss me. I stayed there, holding his hand. It was the first time I felt I loved him entirely. He was so close to my spirit that he became part of me, and I was afraid of him moving further away.

'I love you.'

'And I love you! Forgive me for how I was acting.'

'It's okay … but don't do it again.'

'And if I did?'

'I'd kill you!'

'I'm going to do it again.'

'I'm going to close my eyes. But you'd better not do it again.' I closed my eyes and waited, but he did not kiss me. I opened them back up and found him laughing.

'You know, you're prettier with your eyes closed.'

'Why? Aren't my eyes pretty?'

'No, your eyes drive me wild. But you're even prettier when you close them.'

'You want me to close them?'

'Yes.'

'If you died, I would never close them.'

I picked up my bag, brushed off the dirt, and walked away quickly as he followed behind, pleading with me to wait. I reached the path that led to the park's gate. He hurried to catch up with me, but I ignored him and began singing to myself. He was laughing.

I heard the Baghdad Clock strike ten in the morning. Looking into his eyes, I said, 'I want to go to school. I don't want to miss the entire day.'

Farouq looked at the ground as he said, 'I love you more than the whole world.'

I crossed the street and was nearly run over by a speeding car. I turned back to Farouq to reassure him that I was okay, but he had already gone off in the other direction and was nowhere to be seen.

Everything in my life changed that day. I began feeling that I was a happy young woman, but one who was not innocent and good. I felt a large curtain cutting me off from the world, from Mama and Papa. I was alone in the road, with people watching me through the windows of their cars and saying to themselves, 'This girl has no lips!'

I lifted my fingers to feel my lips, and it seemed that they were bigger than before. I felt a mild pain and imagined they had turned blue. When I reached the school, I went into the bathroom and took a pencil box out of my bag. I opened it and looked at my face in the inside cover, which reflected light as though it were a mirror. My lips looked normal, and there was not any trace of the kiss on them. I went to the deputy head and apologised for my tardiness. She was busy at the time with a pedagogy supervisor who was visiting the school and interrupted me with a gesture to go, so I went to class and sat beside Nadia, who was laughing. I brought my mouth close to her ear and said, 'I have a secret!'

'What?'

'I'm not saying.'

'Tell me!'

I placed a finger over my lips and said, 'Farouq kissed me!'

Nadia smiled with all her heart and said, 'What took you so long?'

'Oh my god, Nadia!'

20

Uncle Shawkat was sent into retirement from his job at the central bank. He no longer had any work to get up for early in the morning. No reason to start the motor of his old car and head off for the day.

He now had a lot of time he did not need. He got up early in the morning but then remembered that he had nowhere to go. He went back and lay his head on the pillow but did not fall asleep.

Getting up again, he went into the kitchen to make breakfast, which he ate while listening to old Iraqi music on the radio, something he had become used to doing every day in his Volkswagen on his way to work.

Uncle Shawkat opened his front gate, stepped halfway out into the street, and smiled at the children on their way to school. Interlacing his hands behind his back, he walked in his pyjamas to the end of the street. He did not know whether he ought to feel any embarrassment because he no longer had any work to do at that hour of the day. Yes. The feeling was getting to him. He was a man with no use. From that day onwards, no one would bring him important papers connected to the movement of currency in the central bank.

Dozens of files had been placed on his desk nearly every day for him to sign after inspecting them to confirm they contained no errors. In recent years, the official papers he had to sign had started running short. He was disgusted by the cash that piled up in high stacks. The currency and its value changed. The paper bills were exchanged for new ones that smelled different. Coins began disappearing: the quarter dinar went away, then the half dinar. Then the dinar itself. The Iraqi dinar disappeared and became a memory from a different time.

He bent his head again in shame when he realised he had gone out into the street in his pyjamas. It was the first time in his life he had done that. He went in and closed the gate. Sitting on his chair in the middle of the garden, he took his retirement letter out of the pocket in which he had put it the night before. He reread it more than once, incredulous that this nearly translucent piece of paper with its four lines had ended his long service, a service which had surpassed a quarter of a century of coming and going every day, to and from work. Addressing Biryad – who sat before him in wonderment that Uncle Shawkat was not going away this morning as he used to do every day – he said, 'This paper, my friend, is like the old currency: a single sheet counts for many and equals a quarter of a century of government service.'

Biryad shook his head and came closer to his owner, who reached down to stroke his back tenderly.

Uncle Shawkat got up and walked around the garden, not knowing what he ought to do. He picked some of the moss that was growing under the pomegranate tree, rinsed his hands under the tap in the garden, and let the water run into the canal. The water poured forth, making narrow channels in the ground and carving a path through the soft dirt of the canal. He saw a small branch resist the flow of water, clinging to a rock that stood in its path in the canal. The branch slipped away, propelled by the force of the gushing water. Uncle Shawkat kept watching until it disappeared from sight. Then he looked at the dog again and said:

'We too, Biryad, are nothing more than little sticks, driven along by the heedless waves of this life. Dry twigs abandoned by their tree and left to lie on the ground of chance. Maybe to be swept away by the flow of a small canal, or to be picked up in the beak of some bird building a nest in that tree. We return home not in our former capacity as branches, but as raw material for the homes of sparrows. Just yesterday I was a green branch in the tree of the workplace, and I've dried up and fallen on the ground, where the water of deadly free time makes sport of me.

'Twenty-seven years, Biryad! I hung on the trunk of a tree that has abandoned me now. How happy that far-off day, when as a young employee I entered the building of the central bank in a suit my father bought in Al-Rashid Street. He also bought me a dark tie and a pair of black shoes from Bata. I sat at my desk and wished in that moment that my mother could see me sitting there on the chair, flipping through important papers on my desk and signing them.

'My mother passed away, my father passed away, and I kept signing papers at my small wooden desk. I fell in love with Nadira. At first, her family rejected me, but she didn't listen to their advice and married me anyway. After years of being united, she left me all alone and went back to them, explaining that life with me had become boring. I no longer went with her to the movies like I did in the old days. It was a long time since we had been to the theatre. We didn't travel to Dohuk, Amadiya and Suwarah Tukah.

'O my dear wife! It wasn't my life that became boring. The whole world became boring. The neighbours you loved are leaving, Nadira. Come, see our neighbourhood: the rusty gates, the neglected gardens buried under the dust of the days. Life isn't as you left it, my wife. Everything here has quickly been transformed.'

A tear rolled down his cheek, and he walked to the bedroom. He changed into his old work clothes, went back into the garden, and got out the lawnmower and his toolbox. With Biryad in tow, he left the house to inspect the houses of the neighbours who had departed. He would double-check that the locks on the doors were secure, and he would look after the plants. He would write on a piece of thick cardboard to hang on this wall or that: house for rent, house for sale.

His suit hung loose these days. He went without his tie. And his shoes needed replacing. There was no longer any space on them for another patch. He exchanged them for an old pair he found in a closet of odds and ends under the stairs. His beard had grown long and become white with depressing black splotches. Uncle Shawkat had begun looking a lot like our neighbourhood.

The sight of beautiful gardens in front of the houses disappeared gradually. Cottages built for recently married children took their place, or small rooms with side doors, rented out for the sake of providing an additional source of income after salaries no longer had any real value.

The green face of our neighbourhood disappeared, and with it, the scent of roses, orange blossoms and grass gradually faded. So too did the fragrance of water when it splashed on the bricks of ancient walls. Our youthful neigh-bourhood had grown up and become old, slowly losing its memory. The number of broken-down cars increased. They choked the streets and impeded the flow of traffic passing through. Rubbish piled up in front of the doors. Teenagers found work to help their families carry the heavy burden of the times.

Bit by bit, the gates became rusty. Windows took on a cloudy hue. Walls facing the street were built higher, as were the walls between neighbouring houses. Iron padlocks were added. Life withdrew into distant rooms. The number of strange faces in the place increased, and the number of thefts went up despite Biryad's barking, which never stopped, day or night. Our houses lost the confidence to seek out what was behind the walls.

21

I have a story I remembered just this moment, and I said to myself I have to tell you about it. It happened one night when Nadia and I were getting ready to take the national aptitude exams. We stayed up in her room to some late hour of the night, when Nadia suddenly threw her book on the floor and leaped up on the bed to dance. I kept my book open and sang for her. Then I gently set it aside and started beating out the rhythm of a song she liked. She jumped down and went to the window, which she opened to look out over the back garden. She breathed in the night air and then came back to start proposing topics that had nothing to do with what we were studying. It was clear she was bored to death.

'I'm sick of studying!'

'It's our final year! Come on, let's finish up and get some sleep.'

'I've had enough! I can't concentrate on books any more.'

She went back and put her hand out of the window to confirm that what she was hearing was raindrops. I knew she had some crazy idea in mind. I have told you before about how much she loves the rain.

'It's raining outside. Let's go out to the street!'

'The street? At this hour? You're crazy!'

'Let's go! I'm so depressed I'll die!'

'What about your parents?'

'Sleeping.'

'And if someone sees us in the street in the middle of the night, what will you say?'

'It's no problem!'

'You have a father, Nadia. Be reasonable for once!'

'If you aren't coming, I'll go by myself!'

I got up too, and we went down the stairs on tiptoes. My heart nearly stopped from fear. With the utmost caution, we opened the door and went out.

We walked down the street at an insane speed. I did not know where she wanted to go at that time of night. The drizzling rain cleaned the air and wet our faces.

'Where are we going?'

'The Baghdad Clock.'

'What will we do there?'

'Take a photo to remember!'

'But we don't have a camera!'

'Don't need one.'

'You're crazy.'

'I know I'm crazy! But I like it. I'm tired of being reasonable.'

'Don't we have exams?'

'We'll be fine!'

As we got closer, we headed in the direction of the clock building. One of the guards was sitting on a small stone bench with his rifle between his knees, listening to a radio that sat beside him under the cement shelter built to protect the bench from the rain. We cautiously passed behind him and went deeper into the darkness, further from the light. We stopped in front of the clock, and Nadia asked me to take an imaginary photo of her. But before I sat on the ground so I could get her and the tower in a single shot, she turned around and, laughing at herself, said, 'Just a minute. Let me make sure Marwa won't show up in the picture!'

I laughed with her and took the photo. She smiled with all her heart and said, 'We've fallen into the future!'

The clock struck midnight in Baghdad, sleeping now under the rain. I put my hand in hers and we ran towards our neighbourhood. We turned into our street and reached her house. Pushing open the door we had left half-open, we slipped furtively into her room on the second floor of the house. We opened our books, but before getting through a single page, we fell asleep on the floor sprawled in opposite directions. Her mother woke us in the morning. We ate a quick breakfast and headed off to school.

The head teacher walked among the graduating classes and, in a tone that was both challenging and encouraging, said, 'This is the school of Mrs Rajaha, and it accepts nothing less than a one hundred per cent success rate.'

These were our last days with Mrs Rajaha and Mrs Athmar in our secondary school, in which we lived through some hard times. They coincided with the years of the sanctions, which deprived us of coloured notebooks and new books. The sanctions placed before our eyes the picture of a future open to possibilities, all of which were unhappy. The familiar faces of our childhood disappeared from their seats in the classroom. Wijdan left us. So did Tabarak, Sumiya and Rita. Absence took many faces away amid the tears. Many names disembarked from the train of our school at many different stops. Someone would disappear, and her absence would linger until the news came that she had emigrated with her family.

Emigration became the defining social characteristic for those who left. The students who stayed felt envy for their classmates who crossed the borders, whose feet touched the ground of a new life, and who breathed the perfume of a new world. Those friends left for cold cities while we disintegrated where we were, living our days of dust with frozen smiles.

22

Khalil went ahead and asked for Shuruq's hand in marriage. Her family assented without the least hesitation. Folk music was performed in the large garden of their house. Candied nuts and other sweets poured down like rain on our heads.

Biryad was the first of the dancers. This was one of his surprises that we had grown used to. From the first note of the large trumpet that a member of the traditional musical troupe had brought, Biryad lifted himself up on his hind legs and began jumping around joyfully in a circle as he wagged his white tail. The musicians were astonished by the sight, something they had never encountered in their work throughout Baghdad's neighbourhoods. When they found that those present did not comment on this strange occurrence, they continued playing, and Biryad continued his delightful dance, which we began to imitate.

The young women went forward, followed by the boys. They moved with a fierce exuberance, for such a long time had passed without happy occasions coming our way that our feet had almost forgotten how to dance. When Biryad saw that the circle had filled with dancers, he brought his front paws down to the ground, lifted his tail over his back, and withdrew without anyone noticing him. He slipped away and reappeared on top of the garden's outer wall and began dancing by himself, watched from the rooftops by cats that were dying with laughter.

A sense of happiness spread everywhere, and spirits relaxed into a sense of joy. The music continued beyond the normal stopping time for this kind of event. Nearly everyone danced, with the exception of Shuruq, who went up to her room after Khalil put the engagement ring on her finger. All alone, the tears began streaming down her face. She did not know why, at this precise moment, her heart went cold and she was more inclined to believe the soothsayer's prophecy regarding the future of her marriage. For when she looked into Khalil's eyes as he put the ring on her finger, she found that his face belonged to another world. Sadness descended on her heart and filled her soul, despite her attempts to hide her true feelings in front of the others.

Khalil's mother, sisters and relatives were perplexed by her lack of emotion at this important occasion in her life, especially when everyone knew the story of love that had joined her to her fiancé. They started thinking it over in their hearts, and when no reasonable answer came to them, they all told themselves the exact same sentence: 'She's overcome with happiness.'

After an hour, Shuruq felt ashamed of her unacceptable absence – at her own engagement party, no less – which would spoil the joy of her family, her fiancé's family and the neighbours. It would provoke rumours about their relationship. She dried her tears, washed her face, lined her eyes with kohl, brushed her hair, and put on a beautiful blue dress that went down to her knees. She had had it altered by the most famous tailor in the neighbourhood and had kept it for this day.

Rather than going down the stairs and joining the party-goers in the garden, her curiosity impelled her to open the door of her small balcony overlooking the garden and to cast a quick glance at the dancers. She saw Biryad dancing on the garden wall and smiled at him when he began wagging his tail at her. She tried to forget everything for the sake of these neighbours and relatives, happy as they were on her day. Before she turned back and closed the balcony door, her eye fell on a strange man dancing and waving his cane with abrupt movements. She focused on his features and let out a muffled scream: 'The soothsayer!'

She hurried down the stairs and out into the garden to grab him and prevent him from getting away, so that she might learn the whole story from him.

She immediately headed towards where the party was going on and pressed her way through to the circle of dancers. She was startled to find the man had disappeared without a trace, even though the dance floor was crowded at that moment with other young men and women, as well as some children from the neighbourhood.

Surprised, she turned back. She asked several women who knew him well, who had spoken with him on his previous visits, but she did not receive any answer. Her question about him was met with disapproving glances and confusion. Some of them even thought the girl had been struck on her engagement day by a mental infirmity from a magic charm placed in her house by one of her rivals.

Shuruq went back to her room and reviewed the chain of events from the first moment this strange person had appeared until his magical disappearance from the dance floor.

Thinking about it exhausted her. She stretched out on her bed and slept till the following morning. When she opened her eyes, she found a doctor gathering up his things to leave amid the deep, confused sadness of her parents and some relatives.

Shuruq rubbed her eyes and, pushing back the heavy covers, got out of bed. She stood there, looking at their faces, asking why they were in her room and why they had called a doctor to treat her.

Meanwhile, a sudden thought popped into her mind that the doctor who had just left bore a remarkable resemblance to the soothsayer. Then she went further and told herself that maybe it was the very same man. Indeed, without a doubt, it was him! 'Him … him … him!' she began repeating at the top of her voice.

Her mother held her and recited in her ear the invocations for warding off evil. Someone brought some cold water to wet her forehead. Shuruq fell onto her bed, shaking like a paper aeroplane in a violent wind. She wrapped herself in the thick blanket and squeezed her eyelids shut.

'Call the doctor!' someone said.

'No, no, no! I don't want a doctor!' Shuruq shouted at the top of her voice from under the covers.

Shuruq was in this state for three days. All attempts by her family to summon the best physicians – including their neighbour, Umm Baydaa, who was a doctor – were of no benefit to her condition. Despite many examinations, no one could diagnose a clear illness in her body.

Wise women, well known for their skill in magic, stood at her bedside, as did wise men expert in the same field. But none of them could give a single clear answer.

After Uncle Shawkat heard the news of her illness – it was on everyone's tongue – he decided to visit her, for from the time he had known her as a small girl and as she had grown up before his eyes into a woman that young men proposed to, she had remained one of the girls in the neighbourhood dearest to his heart. With every step up to her room, it became even more difficult to control the burning tears that fell. They gathered on his eyelashes until they were so big they fell like pebbles, crashing audibly onto the floor. Biryad followed him step by step, smiling with an exuberant happiness that he was entering one of the neighbourhood houses without the slightest feeling of shame.

Uncle Shawkat stood beside Shuruq's bed and sobbed. The dog took advantage of everyone's distraction to move closer without being noticed. Wagging his white tail at the end of her bed where her feet were, he pushed back the covers a little and licked her left ankle.

Uncle Shawkat took her arm. Jokingly, he pressed his teeth in the place of a wristwatch, just as he used to do in the days of her childhood. Shuruq immediately stirred. It was as though the blood began moving through the veins of her desiccated body again. She got up, hugged Uncle Shawkat, and wiped away his tears. She kissed his forehead and asked him to stop crying, for here she was in front of him, safe and sound. Nothing bad had happened to her. In order to prove it, she raised herself to her full slender height on the bed and danced the dance he used to like when she had been a child. He and Baji Nadira would bring her into their house, where she would dance for them as they clapped and kissed her after each dance, pressing a piece of candy into her hand. Her family was surprised at this vigour that flowed through her body and spirit. After the initial shock had passed, her mother let out a trill of joy and summoned her father. Everyone joined them in clapping and calling out expressions of joy and blessing.

Shuruq went back to how she was before and forgot everything connected to the soothsayer and his tales.

Two weeks later, she married Khalil. She lived with him in the cottage she had planned for him, and in her belly, her unborn baby kicked from time to time as she heard the sound of him crying for her. With a mother's tenderness, she would reply, 'Sleep, my little one, sleep!'

Am I Afraid?

23

We graduated from secondary school together with good grades in the final exams. Then we sat at home for a long time, waiting for the results of the central university admissions process. Nadia was accepted into the University of Baghdad, and I was accepted into the University of Technology. This was the first time we would be separated from each other. Nadia kept busy with registration, as did I, and we did not see each other much.

In her dreams now, a new scene kept repeating itself. It was the rising smoke of a war that had settled at the gates, a smoke that reduced visibility, confused everything we saw, and deprived us of our joy at embarking on college life, which we had been looking forward to for so many years.

That was the year of new patriot anthems, the 'year of culmination', as they called it. The atmosphere of war imposed itself anew on our lives, but this war was not like the previous one in that, along with death and destruction, it carried some hope, hope for an end to the sanctions that were crueller than the war itself. The sanctions were a slow death we lived through minute by minute.

The sanctions were not only a weapon to make us starve, they largely put an end to our way of living and destroyed the meaning of life. They stole away the spirit of hope, and when hope disappears, life becomes merely a routine in which we move from one miserable day to another yet more miserable. In such a life, people do not love each other. They do not even love themselves. I saw with my own eyes a woman commit suicide by throwing herself from a bridge into the Tigris. It was during winter, and the water in the river was cold. The people who gathered nearby said that she and her children had not eaten anything for three days, and her husband was in jail for stealing. That incident remained fixed in my mind as the epitome of the sanctions, something that turned a man into a thief bound for prison, while his wife kills herself and leaves their children in the street.

I asked myself what would have happened if that woman had not killed herself. How would she have provided food for her little ones? What would these children have done when they grew up? Every time I thought about what had happened, I imagined what could have been. I would set the woman's husband free from prison immediately; I would find a new job for him; I would bring the woman back from the river; and, putting her hand in the hands of her children, I would make them all go for a walk along the bridge, wearing their best clothes. I would give them one of the abandoned houses in our neighbourhood, bestowing upon them the home that a family had left behind when they emigrated. Then I would ask myself, why did they leave? Would Abu Salli have become a thief if they had not emigrated? Would Umm Salli have killed herself by jumping off a bridge, leaving her daughters to live in the street?

I was afraid I would see another man or woman jump from the bridge. Sometimes I imagined people standing in a long line in front of the bridge, killing themselves in groups, one after another. But what is it that the war will do? Will it end the sanctions? Will those who left come back if the sanctions are dropped? Will Uncle Shawkat become an elegant man again in his dark suit, his white shirt, his blue tie and his shoes? Will Biryad disappear from our lives? Or will he love us more because we give him more food?

On the television, enemy planes were lined up on huge aircraft carriers, and soldiers from all the countries of the world made their way towards us, who welcomed them with patriotic anthems and despair and suicide from the bridge into cold water.

What does the advanced world want from us?

What do these happy countries with their terrifying fleets want from a hungry people in despair and utterly exhausted?

'They have devastated our country and emptied it of the middle class.' Our Arabic teacher repeated this obscure sentence to us every day.

What was the middle class? How did we know if someone belonged to the middle class? This was one of the riddles that confused me. Even when I asked my father, 'Are we in the middle class?' and he answered, 'Yes, because I'm a university professor, and your mother has a master's degree in engineering. We are not rich, but at the same time, we are not poor. We are children of the state, and if our class disappears, the state becomes a broken machine.'

'What about the poor people, father? Aren't they children of the state too?'

He was silent for a while and then looked at me, displeased with my question because fathers need to have answers for every question. 'The poor are the children of the nation,' he told me.

I did not understand politics, and I did not want to understand anything about politics. But I also did not want life in the shelter again. I did not like seeing the buildings collapse onto each other. I did not want the bridges to fall dead into the water. I did not want our house to shake with the rockets crashing into the ground. I did not want to die. I did not want anyone else to die.

Am I afraid?

Yes, I am afraid, very afraid of the war. Afraid even of its declarations, its songs, its music and its patriotic poems. How could I not be afraid when planes hover in the sky and deal out death in straight lines?

Why did I have to witness all this in a single lifetime? A war in my childhood, sanctions as a teenager, and a new war with advanced smart bombs when I have not yet reached twenty. How can a normal person tell their personal life story when they move from one war to another as they grow up?

Is there anything uglier than war? How ugly is this world that understands itself through wars and blockades! What does civilisation mean when we starve children and adults and then launch missiles at them?

What does it mean for humanity to progress when it keeps inventing ever more hideous paths to mutual annihilation?

These are not complicated political questions. They are simply the questions of a person who is afraid. Yes, I am afraid. Deeply afraid, to the point of trembling. My humanity, which hates aircraft carriers, shines forth in this fear. This fear alone forms the foundation of my personal culture, one that hates wars. From this fear, I love all people who tremble in fear at the news of war.

Ahmad was accepted into the Faculty of Architecture at the University of Mosul; Farouq into the College of Sports and Education at the University of Baghdad. We all went our separate ways.

The night before my first day at the university, I rummaged through the old drawer in our living room, looking for the pictures of my mother in her days as a student at the University of Baghdad. I took out one of the photos and brought it up to my room. I knew it well; I had studied it dozens of times. In the photo, my mother was sitting with a group of classmates in the college garden. Nearby sat her friend Fatin, hair done up and looking straight ahead in all her striking, magical elegance.

Aunt Fatin, as I used to call her when I was a child, exemplified what I wanted to be in life. I constantly imagined that when I grew up I would be like her. I would cut my hair like her; I would marry a man who resembled her husband and who worked as an ambassador; I would live with him in the beautiful capitals of the world. Like her, I would meet the wives of ambassadors and diplomats. I would put my hand on my knee and draw my foot in as I turn halfway towards a lady from Africa seated to my right. We would speak about our countries. I would tell her about Iraq, its history, its folklore and its styles. She would tell me about her country. I would listen respectfully and nod my head at every word.

I looked at the photo carefully, engrossed in the details: her shirt, her skirt, her shoes and socks. For a long time, I studied the way she sat and how her hands were folded on her knee as she smiled like a princess from some elegant time. Fatin was a beautiful student from the time of my beautiful mother, that era that breathed magnificence and self-confidence, when being a university student meant being a smart young woman, armed with knowledge and strength of personality; it meant self-reliance and confidence in the world. I stuck the photo on the right side of my mirror frame and began arranging my clothes and adjusting my hair under her guidance, wanting to be like her.

I put on my skirt and found that it was longer than hers. I put on my socks, which were a darker colour than her socks. I put on my shoes, which were embarrassed and reluctant. I did my hair, but it did not come out as I wanted. A great space of time stood between Aunt Fatin and me, time that changed things and made that way of life distant. The picture of Fatin belonged to a future the city had left behind, a future that stopped there, floating in place in the form of old photo albums forgotten in the drawer.

I left my clothes on the edge of the desk and went to sleep.

The next morning, I woke up to a new sun, a warm sun that sent its rays into my soul. That day I became a university student. I became part of real life, part of the delicious days I had imagined. On my own, I struck out from my family to live in a new world that spread before me all at once.

University life was not just a stage of advanced study; it was life in all its earnestness. Old relationships were broken up and formed anew. From the very first, what it meant to be a classmate was different. The meaning of relationships with others was different. Things became clearer; mistakes were no longer innocent. From this morning on, the right to be wrong would be a foreign concept. The right to be spontaneous was disallowed. The right not to bear responsibility for our behaviour, in its turn, would seem bizarre.

I stepped timidly through the university gates. In that moment, I imagined that all eyes were turned upon me, watching. Every mouth was talking about me, just as though I had suddenly been born into a strange world. I heard my shoes strike the pavement and focused my gaze on the ground so as not to lose my balance.

Whenever a fleeting laugh reached my ears, I choked on the pain inside. I was sure my feet would stumble on the uneven pavement and I would fall. I had forgotten my old way of walking, which I had practised ever since my first steps on the rug at home. How had I run down the neighbourhood alleys all those years without ever being afraid of falling?

The first day of university was the clear division between two times in my life: the time of innocent playing in naive childhood and happy adolescence, and a new time when everything inside me contracted. It was as though my nerves had stiffened under the mockery of people's faces, their actions and reactions. I no longer had an answer ready for every question. It was necessary to think carefully about every word I uttered. It was necessary to watch my steps, to feign assurance and to sit cautiously in the lecture hall.

Do I carry my books in my right hand or my left? Do I put my bag on the floor, or do I keep it beside me? Do I sit up on the front of the chair, or do I lean back? Do I move my hands freely when I sit down, or do I hold them still on my lap? How could I have forgotten to ask my mother all these questions? Why had I relied on my spontaneity to carry me through?

Everyone here had friends who came from the same secondary school or from the same neighbourhood they had lived in. I was the exception. I was the only one who walked alone. I sat on a small bench in the shade. I was too embarrassed to buy anything to eat, and I became confused if anyone looked in my direction.

Some days later, I discovered by chance that Baydaa was a student in the same university, though in a different department. My soul clung to her, and I sought her out between lectures. I would sit with her in the student centre far from the others. She would reminisce with me and sing with a voice that I alone heard.

Baydaa alone came here with me from our neighbourhood. She was the message that reached me from a secure past. In those days, Baydaa represented for me the nineteen years that were my entire life. With her, I was like someone grasping her mother's hand while taking a step into cold, deep water. It was as though the university was a cold river whose temperature I tested with a finger before throwing myself in.

'My friend, where have you been all this time! How have you been, my dear?'

I held back a tear and murmured, 'I miss secondary school so much.'

'The time will come when you will miss university.'

My mind wandered off, overcome by memories of the old days. Then our time was up. I kissed her cheek as though I were kissing the entire neighbourhood, kissing nineteen years of my childhood when we ran across the playground grass towards our classroom.

Baydaa was a young woman with a child's face, clear skin, and grey eyes with thick eyebrows that joined above her small nose. With her good heart and generous emotions, she lived life exuberantly. On days when I was too busy to visit her, she would come to my department and seek me out like the mother of a single daughter who feared the air might do something to her beloved girl. She would kiss me with the tenderness of a thousand grandmothers kissing the soul of their only grandson. With her alone I felt I was still living in our neighbourhood, on our street, attending our old school.

Each time we parted, Baydaa walked with me, and we made our way along the narrow path imprinted by students' feet on the damp grass. We stood in the middle of the campus, halfway between the architecture department and the civil engineering building. We were only one step apart, but in my mind, that step represented my childhood and my adolescence.

Once when I was waving goodbye, I stumbled and fell onto the ground. Another girl reached down and helped me to my feet. I brushed off my skirt, thanked her, and continued on my way with a new tear in my eye.

24

I did not think too much about the soothsayer who had arrived in our neighbourhood once upon a time and had become the subject of everyone's conversation. By my own intuition, I knew everything he said. Even before he spoke of it, I had seen the ship on that day I climbed up on the water tank. I knew we were living in a dangerous ocean. I did not care what he was talking about. I just kept wishing that some young soothsayer would come in his place, perhaps his daughter, his sister or some other relative. Or even a stranger he did not know. A teenage soothsayer in fine clothes who would put her right hand on her forehead to take her temperature from time to time, and then would be silent for two minutes before picking up where she had left off.

I would not want her to summon good luck for me or tell me about my future children. What I dreamed was that she would answer questions that had to do only with the past. Not the events that had taken place, for those I remembered well. But the important thing was to know how some of these events had happened. And what if some of them had not? Among these questions, there were some that seemed ridiculous, and others that were important. But it is a question of degree, and the answers to silly questions often bring us to an understanding of life's most important and complicated matters.

Well, to give an example, one thing I wanted to know was why Farouq loved me and not any of the other girls of the neighbourhood, or any of the girls he had met in his life who loved him or found him attractive.

Why did I become Nadia's friend from our first meeting in the shelter, even though there were other girls our age who came every night with their families, whom we ignored from the first moment we met each other?

What if there had never been a war? What if the sanctions had not been put in place? What would our lives have been like, and what would Baghdad have become?

Questions like these were the crazy things that ran through my mind. They were the ones that would lead me to true answers about the deep, hidden meanings. They would let me know the meaning of love, friendship, chance and history, and how events come to be.

I imagined this young soothsayer as she passed by our street without Biryad barking at her. On the contrary, he would go up to her, smell her hand, and then move aside to clear a way for her, giving me a sign through his welcome.

It would happen that she would pass by when I was standing alone at the gate of the house. I would approach and invite her in to our garden to sit on the swing. I would sit on the grass in front of her and ask my questions.

'Why did Farouq love me and not the other girls of the neighbourhood or the girls he met throughout his life? Why did Nadia fall in love with Ahmad and no one else? And why was Marwa attached to him alone?'

Raising her right hand to feel her forehead, the soothsayer would fall silent for two minutes and then answer as she turned her head to look around the garden: 'Listen, my dear. If people knew why they fell in love, they wouldn't fall in love at all. And if it were granted to them to know why they loved one person and not any other, they wouldn't love them in the first place.

'Love, my friend, is in the category of things that are not made in this life of ours. It existed before us and will go on after us. Love is not some physical part of our bodies or any raw material found in nature. It is not a chemical reaction or a physical element. It is not a property of geography, not a historical event; neither a mathematical equation nor an engineering hypothesis.

'The question about the meaning of love is the same question as the meaning of our existence. It will forever remain a question with no clear answer. For this reason, our ancient ancestors invented the goddesses Ishtar, Inanna, Venus and Adonis, Aphrodite, Cupid and others. They invented many goddesses in order to spare themselves the trouble of this question, for everything that the goddess makes, the goddess alone answers for, and rarely do goddesses make humans their partners in their special domain.

'You exist if you fall in love.

'Imagine you lived without lungs. Would air have the same meaning it has now? Love is air that doesn't need lungs. Imagine you did not have eyes. Would things have the same clarity? Love is something whose existence we see without eyes, that we hear and taste and touch without any physical sensations. There is a single sense for love, which is ourselves – our entire existence, with and without our five senses. Love is the spiritual light in our depths, and light, as you know, has no mass. It has no tangible material, yet it exists. It exists even in the meaning of darkness itself. The question about light's mass is fundamentally a simple question of physics. The one about love remains an incomplete sentence, even if we add a thousand question marks.'

The soothsayer would ask me for a little water. I would go inside to bring her a large glass, in which I would put a little ice so that she would not need to ask for that too.

Talking with her was an invaluable opportunity not to be relinquished, even if her responses did require deep concentration, given that she would sometimes speak without saying anything. I imagined bringing her the glass. She took a drink and set it down beside her.

'Why did I become Nadia's friend from the first meeting in the shelter, even though there were other girls of our age who came every night with their families, whom we ignored from the moment we first got to know each other?'

She did not put her hand to her forehead as I had been expecting her to do. She shifted in her seat, and her eyes wandered through the garden, as though she were listening to the plants. She focused her gaze on the fig tree. Then she turned to me and said, 'Friendship resembles love in some respects, but the goddess has left it to humans in their freedom. Friendship in its nature does not come from a glance, a smile or a letter expressing admiration. Friendship grows naturally and develops over time. It replaces natural differences between friends with agreement.

'Friendship allows room for an unlimited number of people, varying in degree from one friend to another according to your ability to become acquainted with a thousand friends without any one of them calling you a traitor.

'You and Nadia do not love each other just for the sake of the deep friendship between you. You love your memories too.

'Both of you, but especially you, are afraid for these memories, because their passing means ripping up the solid ground under your feet. For those who fear the future, the past is a merciful cave in which people seek shelter when they turn away from the cruelty of the present.

'Friendship is an unambiguous human blessing, and what's more, it is holier than love in that it does not require any kind

of worship or renunciation of dignity, as does the latter. By
its nature, friendship leaves an appropriate distance between
friends, clear boundaries that must not be crossed. In addition
to all that, it is not egotistical in a way that prevents the other
from living their life however they wish.'

I considered her words and thought to myself, 'This
soothsayer is a devil. She speaks well, but what she says is
not necessarily true.' I thought I would end the conversation
with her, but I had skipped some questions, and I asked the
one about war and the sanctions.

'What if there had never been a war? What if the sanctions
had not been put in place? What would our lives have been
like, and what would Baghdad have become?'

'Well,' said the soothsayer, 'that's a very good question.'
She passed her right hand over her forehead, was silent for
a couple of minutes, and then continued: 'Listen, my dear.
I know you want to say, "Were it not for the war and the
sanctions, things would have been better for us." That might
be true, if we were to ignore geography and history. For you
are a victim of geography in the first place. Your country
isn't on the Mediterranean where it might breathe the sea
air, nor is it in the desert, where it might live on the luxury
brought by oil. You live halfway between them, where the
bright light of the sun shines down on you all year round.
Which is good on the one hand, but light resembles utter
blindness, for it prevents the accumulation of dreams. Look
into the eyes of any European, for instance, and you'll find
an obscure story, while in the eyes of any Iraqi, you get the
whole thing immediately in a single sentence. The sun dries
up ideas like it dries shirts on a clothes line. That's why you
don't accumulate ideas and preserve your dreams. These
words of mine may seem strange to you, but they're the
truth. Modern civilisations are found in winter climes where

the bright sun rarely shines. Bright light deprives souls of depth. This is the part connected with geography.

'As for what's attached to history, you are the children of a long, disconnected history. Your countries live through the ages as islands separate from each other. The history of pain alone is the sole river flowing through your time. You and sadness form an eternal friendship, and whenever its river dries up, you fill it up again with your tears. To tell the truth, I don't know if it is you who are chasing sadness, or whether sadness is following you. You are masters at producing sorrow but ignorant of the alphabet of joy. Look at your songs and your music. Look at your tears when you laugh. Look at your poems and your proverbs. With you, even love is an allusion to sadness, absence, anguish and separation.'

'What's the solution?'

'Geography is a fate that cannot be escaped, but history is made. Adapt to your geography and change your history.'

'How do we change history? Do you mean falsify it?'

'Not at all. Just weave from its cloth a new garment. Gather the good islands together and leave out the painful ones. There, make a fresh memory, a good space for joy. In short, change the entire culture. Or at least some of it.'

'I don't understand what you're saying!'

'It's not important that you understand. That may take a long time. But write down my words and preserve them for your children. Preserve them for the future.'

Saying that, she got up to leave. She smiled at me and asked for the silver bracelet on my wrist with my name written in small letters, as a memento of me that she would keep forever. She said goodbye, and I closed the gate behind her. Biryad, who had been hiding on top of the garden wall, jumped down and headed towards his owner's house. Had he been eavesdropping on us? Who knows?

25

To stumble and fall when you are a college student is not the same as when you are in primary or secondary school. Childhood is a time for experiments, when we learn how to get back up quickly after a fall. As we get older, we learn that we are never supposed to stumble. Thus, with the passage of time, we lose the freedom even to trip.

I thanked the student who reached out and helped me up when I fell on the campus grass, but I continued on my way without looking back. In my embarrassment, I decided not to go to the lecture hall, but instead headed away, far from the eyes of the students. I sat alone on a secluded bench and nearly choked on my tears.

Was Farouq an emotional fall on the road of my adolescence? Did I have to get up and brush off the skirt of my memories this time? Was I in need of a new life, a life that began this very moment and plunged into the future?

No, I told myself, it is not like that. Farouq is the truth that ties me to my beautiful time. He is the link that connects me to myself, to my world in our neighbourhood, to my songs, to the emotions I recall.

Farouq is the first word, the first touch of the hand, the first kiss. He is the first embarrassment, the first mistake, the first risk. He is the white gull that lands at my window in the morning, and he brought the sun into my life when he told me, 'I like you,' going on to say, 'I love you,' when I became tongue-tied and did not reply.

The first admiration that someone shows you is the truest kind, born without any history. It is the unexpected event that we receive just as it is, without any preparation, and we preserve it in our memories forever.

That first admiration is a sublime spiritual language, in which we consecrate a new era in the civilisation of love, that vast kingdom that builds its towers, its ziggurats, and its hanging gardens in young hearts.

Many weeks passed, during which I met my prince just once, briefly. I ran into him by chance in the street, and we walked through the neighbourhood alleys. We did not have much to talk about at the time. Together, we sang all the songs we knew. Our old songs alone afforded us that singular feeling of intoxication and insensibility.

My university books did not resemble my old books. They were entirely free of scribbles, free of the cryptic phrases I would record for myself so that others would not understand, those words I used to write unconsciously. My notebooks too were free of the letter F, which I used to draw big in different colours. Had I begun thinking about the future?

We do not fear the past because everything that can happen has happened, and it remains at our memory's disposal. We dread the future.

Is it possible that Farouq will become a story of the past? Could Nadia someday become part of the past? Ever since Nadia entered the University of Baghdad and I joined the University of Technology, fear had grown within me. I feared for our friendship, that the future would steal it from our hands. How did she and I not go each morning to the same school, enter the same class, and sit at the same desk? How did we not study together? Not invent excuses to tell each other's parents and the deputy head, Mrs Athmar? How would we walk home from the main street without being together? What would Biryad say when he saw me alone, without Nadia? Would he recognise me?

Would the future take her from me? With the passage of time, would she become just an old friend with whom I reminisced about the air-raid shelter, school, the Baghdad Clock and Al-Zawra when we ran into each other? What would I do about her dreams, which I was addicted to watching?

I would sometimes run into her at the end of the street, waiting for her bus when I was there for a different one. We would talk a little, and then one of the buses would come before the other and end our conversation. She would go to Al-Jadriya, and I would go to Al-Sana'a Street. It was not far, but neither was it close.

The future was coming – so brash and careless – and it would make our generation old: old songs, old clothes, even an outdated dialect. Dear God, we too were growing old! The wars had kept us busy, and we forgot that we were growing up. The modern wars retained their vigour as we advanced in age. The rockets were still young as we passed into distant years.

Time would surprise us. Hatem Al-Iraqi would become an old singer. Haitham Yousif too, and Muhannad Mohsen, Raid George and Ismail Al-Farwaji. Adnan would get old, Lena would get married, and Sinbad would retire from sailing the Seven Seas. Our dialect would change, and our words would appear strange. Customs, in turn, would evolve, and standards would be inverted. With the shift in our local dialect, everything would be different. For a dialect is the repository of morals and the guiding force of a people's behaviour. When we give it up, we lose ourselves and our feelings become distorted.

Every day at university, I heard new, somewhat strange, words. Words entirely lacking in courtesy. Words with sharp letters that squeezed themselves into the way we spoke and tried to penetrate the memory of our Arabic dialect. Even more, they warned of a deep spiritual ruin. By its nature, a local dialect develops spontaneously, responding to an inner growth. With the passage of time, it continually transforms reality and then refashions itself.

In the hallways at college, in class, at the student centre, I lived as a stranger among strangers. I was not myself, the way I was in my old school, in my neighbourhood, at home. I was now forced to become reacquainted with myself. I was presenting others with a false impression of this student who was me; I was reduced to a series of fake copies of myself.

Is that right? Maybe.

No, I'm wrong. I am here at university now. I am clearer about who I am, more at peace with myself. I pose dozens of complicated questions to myself, and hear dozens of simple answers in response.

In the beginning, in the first days of university life, I was somewhat afraid of the students I did not know: normal, understandable fears of what is new and different.

We are instinctively afraid of things we do not know. We fear the uncertainty produced by first impressions: this young man, good to the point of naivety; this unfortunate young woman; this wicked student; this deluded girl; this mean clique; this complicated classmate; this haughty man; this humble woman; this upright young man. At first, these evaluations of others take place without any experience, and then little by little, things become clearer. Time guarantees the foolishness of our first impressions. Why did we have to form first impressions anyway? Why did we not let time do its thing without getting entangled with others or entangling them with ourselves?

Only with Baydaa did I feel reassured. That was not because my first impression of her had been good, but because of time, which was responsible for combatting the darkness that obscured the nature of her soul. Time was what made me so attached to her. Time was what piled up between us in the shape of memories.

Should I transfer and join Baydaa's course in order to stay close to her?

What if Baydaa herself had changed? What if she no longer loved her memories?

That morning, I spoke to Nadia about her as we waited for the bus. 'Baydaa studies in a department close to mine,' I told her, 'and I go to meet her between lectures.' Nadia was not very interested and did not make any comment. It appeared that she no longer lived in semi-exile at her college. She did not experience what it means to announce one's presence among people, as though suddenly born without any history.

Nadia was acting differently towards me that morning. Actually, she was not behaving in her usual way at all. This girl had grown up a lot, more than her age would suggest. She had put a layer of foundation on her face, and the make-up concealed her old freshness from me. The layer of colour was relatively pronounced, and she did not need so much of it. Nadia in her natural state was more beautiful than Nadia with make-up.

But what is this natural state in which she is more beautiful? The one I saw when I confined her to an eternal box, where I wanted to keep her because she was all my memories? I knew Nadia when she was small, the person I met in the air-raid shelter. I grew up with her in primary and secondary school. I was the friend of her childhood and her adolescence, and this make-up was an intruder in our relationship. It brought her to a new world far away from me. Make-up was a practice hostile to our memories. It was just a pale way of making peace with the present, or a stupid way of distorting the past. Or else it was a feeble weapon to delay the future's betrayal.

Farouq surprised me once with a strange gift, one I was not expecting from him. After he came back from a trip with the youth national team, he gave me a multi-tiered box of make-up. The colours varied gradually from dark brown to light pink. It was the first time in my life I possessed that kind of box, the first time I discovered that my face could be threatened by strange colours. I went up to my room and began experimenting. I put red, blue and green on my cheeks and under my eyes until I looked like a clown. I had previously seen my mother put a little white moisturiser on her face. Then she would take a light red pen and pass it over her lips. But not all these colours. Once I went secretly into her room, sat on the chair she would sit on as she made herself up, and began playing around with her powders in front of the mirror. All of a sudden she entered the room, took me by the hand, and laughed at me in front of my father. He took me on his lap and said, 'When you grow up, you'll put make-up on your face and be beautiful.'

Was Farouq trying to tell me I was beautiful?

Was I not beautiful without these colours?

Farouq was not thinking about it the way I was. Maybe he wanted to tell me I had become a woman.

Farouq… You too have become a man. You no longer write me letters that you colour and sprinkle with cologne. You have begun bringing gifts like television stars do, new gifts from the world of adults.

I did not take the bus for female students that day but decided I would go to meet Farouq. Today I will leave the future to everyone else and walk towards the past. I will go walking with Farouq through streets that know me, that I know. I do not want to enter the future. I am afraid of the past disappearing. I am afraid of the unknown. The future is open to all possibilities, and each possibility on the horizon these days frightens me. There are no miracles that the future will realise. It is a sick old man leaning on the crutch of the past as he comes towards us.

The future is not a swift road that carries us forward. That is nothing more than a foolish and trivial lie. We live aboard an enormous ship. The waves push it around aimlessly. Storms batter it amid the heaving sea of the world's madness. How can we be confident of the future if we do not move forward? How can we submit our affairs to it when we are falling behind? How many times have we left our future behind and become lost on the road to ourselves?

The past is the only truth I am certain of. I know it well, and I find reassurance even in its destruction. I have a vague dread of what is coming. It is a deep feeling of defeat, a frantic sense that we are passing into chaos. Everything crashes down before our eyes; the fruits of the future rot on the vine and fall to the ground. They seduce me with a bitter taste and an obscure, unknown fate, and I look out towards wide horizons shrinking like a narrow alley in an old Baghdad neighbourhood. I saw that once in Nadia's dream, and I have not forgotten it since.

I will go out with Farouq this evening. I will wander with him along the paths of the past. I will recall with him all the stories that have nothing more to tell. I will speak to him in the dialect I love, a dialect that contains all that I am as a person. Who are we apart from the language we speak?

26

War was coming. There was no longer any possible doubt about it. We all knew it; we breathed it in the air. Without any contact, its magnetic force shifted things out of place. We moved like iron filings under the influence of its negative charge, having lost all sense of direction.

Up on the roof of our house, I stood on the water tank a second time, inspecting our ship and its high sails on the distant horizon. I rubbed my eyes and watched for war, the goals of which I could define precisely. I have become an expert on this place, an expert on war and its ends. I know exactly what it sought.

Come along, war, my old friend! This is Ma'mun Tower; this is the Baghdad Clock. The tall buildings are over there, and that is the airport. Go to Al-Rashid Street, where towers and buildings wait for you. Try the Bridge of the Republic, where you will find a tall building called the Ministry of Planning. Come over this way and drop your payload here. Turn back a little. There is the power station, and not far from it is the big water tank. Come a little closer and drop your bombs on us. Throw down your burden anywhere you like. This time, you stand alone in the arena. We are exhausted and in despair. Come, get rid of us like human scraps, superfluous to this world. We too no longer have any need of it.

A squadron of birds moves across the sky. I lift my eyes and turn my face towards the arc of their flight, longing for their lightness. How happy are these creatures who live without country. I want to fly with them, to soar far away. I want to live in a new world, a world without wars. O heavens, be good to me just this once! I have become tired of our homeland.

Our primary school was turned into a military barracks. The middle school became a missile depot. Anti-aircraft guns were erected on top of the secondary school, their muzzles circling the sky.

Nadia came to our house looking for me. She found me on the roof, watching for the war. 'Come on!' she said, taking me by the hand and leading me towards the garden. 'I want to spend this night in the shelter. I want to live there again. Last time, I was a child and did not understand what it means for people to run away from death. Come with me tonight.'

'Have you gone mad, Nadia?'

'No, not at all. I just want to experience the meaning of running away from death.'

'But the war hasn't begun. The shelters are locked.'

'Come on; let's just try! Let's race war and laugh in its face. If nothing else, let's try running away from life.'

I went out with her on a scouting mission to find the shelter. The concrete building was surrounded with barbed wire, the dust of twelve years of neglect piled up against it. Stray dogs and starving cats slept in its shadow.

Twelve years had passed since we met in this desolate place. No one at all had been inside since the last night we had spent there. The country no longer needed air-raid shelters; fleeing death was no longer a vital matter. The important thing now was escaping life. Nadia squeezed through the barbed wire, and I followed. I matched her steps as she headed for the small door we used to go through.

We reached the narrow staircase where we used to play as children. She stood up to her full height on the fifth step and leaped through the air. When her feet hit the floor, she clapped for herself in delight. She urged me to jump too, and I stood on the same step. I pretended to be afraid and walked down, laughing at how crazy she was. Then I went back up and jumped into the air.

She went up and jumped a second time, then a third and a fourth without getting tired of it. When I begged her to stop this game so that we might leave this murky hole with its damp smell, she ignored me and pressed on deep into the shadows of the place. I followed her with frightened steps.

In the corner where we had slept in 1991, we found a wide wooden bed. Beside it was a clay jar of water dripping a wet trail, a long staff, sunglasses, a pocket watch, a medicine bottle and an old book with a torn cover. Confused, we advanced towards the bed. A man was sleeping there, but not snoring. There was no sound of breathing or a beating heart. We got very close, but he remained motionless as a rigid corpse, wrapped in a white sheet that went up over his head. As Nadia hesitated and was about to uncover his face, he surprised her by throwing back the sheet and laughing loudly.

The soothsayer!

He leaned forward with a dead smile on his face. Then he took out a flashlight hidden under his pillow and shone the light in our eyes, laughing so hard he could not catch his breath.

'Don't be afraid,' he told me. Then he shone the light in Nadia's eyes and said, 'Don't be afraid.'

We felt a kind of reassurance that eased our fear somewhat. The soothsayer swung his legs off the bed and addressed me. 'I know you're not anxious to know what's coming, but now, this instant, is the time when I send you to a city beyond the future.' He corrected himself to say, 'I will send the two of you to an afterlife.'

I got a little closer to him and said, 'Before you send us anywhere, you have to tell us who you are. How did you come into the neighbourhood? Why did you choose us and no one else? Who sent you? What is your aim in all this? Do you know that ever since the day you appeared among us, we have not known a moment's peace?'

The soothsayer leaned back against the headboard and began to laugh. Then he cleared his throat and said, 'That's a lot of questions. How can I answer them all at once? I don't usually answer questions like these, but nevertheless, I'll tell you one thing. You, personally, have heard it before. Do you remember the captain you met on the ship's deck one night?'

'Yes, I remember that well.'

Nadia came closer, surprised to hear these words, and before she could utter a sound, I told her, 'I'll explain it all later. It's complicated, but I'll tell you all about it.' Then I repeated my response to the soothsayer: 'Yes, I remember that well.'

'Good, my little one. I am just an idea in the neighbourhood's imagination. The neighbourhood is just an idea in my head. Everything our eyes fall upon is only an idea, and there's nothing real about reality. We are all imprisoned in our imaginations, and our experiences actually consist only of ideas. Existence as a whole is a collection of ideas. That is the sole truth. Don't believe anything else, and don't tell it to anyone because people don't believe things that don't occur to their minds independently. They don't know where their minds reside, and there's never a day when they ask themselves whether they really possess something called a mind. What's it like? What colour is it? The mind, my little one, is just another idea, a complicated idea made from others as though they were all true.'

I remembered these words, the exact ones I had heard from the captain, and here was the soothsayer repeating them to me. Was he the captain? I thought about asking him that, but he did not give me the chance. He shone the flashlight into Nadia's eyes, and when he had fixed it precisely on her pupils, he drew her in forcefully and launched her far away into a world of light. Then he turned and did the same thing to me.

I entered an expansive city. Its walls were built with bricks made of faint sunlight. Passing under an arch of white neon light, the kind that might come from a nearby star, I carefully picked my way down a narrow path paved with red stones that glowed from within as though they were cubes of ice. Swallows with golden wings flew towards me. At the end of the path a magnificent gate opened up, leading into an enormous hall whose ceiling nearly touched the stars. Exhilarating perfumes wafted from each corner of the room.

A small swallow separated from its flock and approached me. It led me towards a side room made of intense light, where it bade me sit on a sofa that was nearly the same as the one we had in our house, though this one was made of translucent glass. It was in the middle of a large room through which a cool breeze was blowing.

The bird went out, flapping its bronze wings, and left me there by myself. I did not know what awaited me in that strange and desolate place.

Hours passed, maybe days, while I remained as I was, still sitting there. When I got hungry, some strange kind of fruit dropped down from a tree with a red pastel trunk, and whose branches were yellow, blue, green, purple and so on, with no end to the different shades of colour. I tried to remember how I got there, but I no longer knew anything outside this world of light apart from my memory of this sofa. I heard the voices of my parents, calling me from far away, but there was no air in my lungs to reply.

The door opened, and the swallow passed through, leading Nadia in. It gave a sign for her to sit beside me. She sat on the far end of the sofa, as though surprised at my presence, or as though she did not recognise me. She began examining my features in order to remember me but did not succeed. I looked at her and tried to say, 'Hi, Nadia,' but again, the lack of air in my lungs stopped me.

A white angel with wings too small for its body came walking by on delicate feet. With a gesture of its left wing, it commanded us to follow and led us into a large courtyard. Faint stars glittered in the sky. Enormous circles of deep darkness spread in the distance. We passed through dim streets, turning dozens of times to skirt forests of bright trees that shifted around us and changed their direction with each turn. A long way off, we saw a small cottage built into the side of a green hill surrounded on three sides by cypress trees. Shooting stars with strange light descended towards it.

The door to the cottage opened, and a young woman, twenty years old, welcomed us. She was wearing a yellow sash and shoes made of feathers. On her wrist she wore a silver bracelet engraved with my name. A white cat followed her. She guided us through the small rooms of the cottage until we reached the kitchen, where she said there was enough food to keep us alive for many centuries.

With its kitchen and other rooms, the cottage resembled those country homes you see in movies, where the snow falls no matter what time of year it is.

The young woman nodded in farewell. Leaving the cat with us and giving us an ambiguous smile, she went out. Nadia sat on a seat covered in feathers, and I sat on another nearby. She smiled at me, and I smiled at her. Air filled my chest again, and I yelled, 'Nadia!' before rushing forward to embrace her. The white cat came over to us and jumped up in Nadia's lap. It was our cat, the very one we had brought home after we found it shivering from the cold.

Nadia and I sat with the cat between us. We talked late into the night, establishing a new memory in this new world. We lay down on the colourful rug and closed our eyes. Nadia began talking to herself and smiling. I knew she was dreaming. I came close, put my face in front of hers, and began to watch her dreams. But this time she prevented me and shut the door to her dreams in my face.

In the morning, a small star rose up through the window and told us he was the child of the sun. The swallow landed on a branch and veiled the star with its wing.

Someone knocked on the door. Nadia got up to answer it, and the girl who had welcomed us the night before came in. Nine beautiful girls were with her, one of whom resembled Mayada when she was a teenager. Trailing shining white garments and wearing yellow sashes, they came over to greet us. I got up and went into the kitchen to make them tea. The girl who looked like Mayada followed me to make sure I was able to use everything in the kitchen, and when she found I knew my way around, she asked, 'Do you know Dr Tawfiq?'

'No, I don't believe I've ever heard that name.'

'His clinic is in the main street. Please go and tell him that Mayada loves him and is waiting for him here.'

'I'll do it,' I told her.

She kissed me and went into the sitting room, where she stood, watching from afar. The girls had begun speaking to Nadia as though they were old friends come to welcome her. I brought them tea, which they drank with coordinated movements as though they were a ballet troupe performing a mime.

After several minutes, an old man came in, leaning on a staff that he used to push open the door. He took a small piece of paper out of his pocket and read off Nadia's name. He told her to stand. 'You will go back whence you came.'

He went towards her, took her by the hand, and went out. I remained alone with the cat, looking into the faces of the young women. The one wearing the silver bracelet went out. One by one, the rest followed her with sad faces and closed the door on me.

'I want to go back!' I screamed at the top of my voice.

A man in his mid-forties appeared and looked through the window with a smile.

'I want to go back,' I told him.

He kept smiling without moving away, and I began shouting at him. After a while, he went towards the door and pushed it open. He came inside and said in scolding tone, 'Where is it you want to go back to?'

'To our house. To my parents. To our neighbourhood. To my friends. To the university I want to attend with Nadia. I want Baghdad…'

'What will you do amid that ruin, with war at its gates?'

'What would I do here in this desolate place, with no air in my lungs?'

'It's because you…'

'What? Because I'm dead?'

'No, you're in-between.'

'What do you mean?'

'You are in a place between life and death. We examine the names here to confirm the dead before they die.'

'And am I among them?'

'Not yet.'

'How long will I remain like this?'

'Until we know your name. Up until now, you haven't mentioned your name to us, and we haven't been able to come across it in the records. We don't know anything about you.'

I took several steps towards him and whispered my name in his ear. He asked me to repeat it, and I did. 'My God!' he said. 'I know you. I know your family well. They are my family too, and I love them. I am Ahmad's father. Do you know him?'

'Yes, I know him and his mother too. Are you the one who was martyred in the Iraq–Iran War?'

'Yes, that was me. Before I died, I was your neighbour, and your parents were my friends. I love them. How are they doing? How is my wife, and my young son Ahmad?'

'They are all doing well. Ahmad is no longer young. He is now studying engineering at the University of Mosul. He loves Nadia, who just left.'

'Has he really grown up? And experienced love too?'

'Yes. He is a handsome young man who loves life. Nadia loves him with all her heart.'

'What joy to be in love and live out a love story in Baghdad!'

'What do you mean, Uncle? Baghdad is no longer as you knew it.'

'I know; I know it well. But we love it, and we only see it as we imagine it. Come! Your grandfather lives with me in that glass palace on the other side. I got to know him here years ago. He is a good and generous man. We call him Harun al-Rashid.'

His words struck me with confusion. I longed to see my grandfather, but I was afraid he would keep me with him. I wanted to ask Abu Ahmad why they called him Harun al-Rashid, but he interrupted my thoughts by saying, 'Your grandfather loves Baghdad. He loves its people. He loves the workshops and the interlacing streets. Even here, in this blessed life, he does not drink the pure water but asks for water that has been brought from the Tigris River. Look at that wall around his house. Do you see it? He built it himself with bricks made from Baghdad clay, calling it the Baghdad Wall. When evening comes and he trembles with desire, he goes to Baghdad in the time of the Abbasid Caliphate and wanders through its palaces before sitting in the place of Harun al-Rashid, summoning the poets and sages so he might listen to them. Then he calls for singers and musicians to stay up all night with them until the morning. He doesn't want Baghdad to sleep.'

'But why Harun al-Rashid? Wasn't Al-Mansur the one who build Baghdad?'

'Harun al-Rashid is a Baghdadi idea, a dream that its people dream. *The Baghdad of Harun al-Rashid* is a story the city tells about itself. The truth or falseness of the tale is not the important thing.'

'Yes, I see that now,' I told him, although in fact I did not understand very well what he was saying.

He took a piece of yellow paper out of his pocket, read it, and said, 'Wait here a while. I'll come back and set you free from this place.'

I sat waiting for more than an hour. It may have been more than a day, or less. I do not know how much time I was waiting for him because they do not have time there, no clocks that look like the Baghdad Clock and count out the seconds. Abu Ahmad came back in the military uniform he had been wearing when he died and accompanied me to a dwelling made of glass that stretched to the horizon without an end. My grandfather lived there.

There was a large sunlit garden, shaded by leafy trees. My grandfather was sitting on a chair made of aluminium with colourful strips of plastic. In his lap was the small white cat. He was wearing the same clothes and glasses I had seen in the picture hanging on the wall of my grandmother's room. Beside him was an old box that bore the stamp of Mackintosh's Candies, in which shaving implements were carefully arranged. On a small bench beside him sat a man I did not recognise. He dipped a small shaving brush in a bowl of shaving cream and then spread it over my grandfather's face. Having finished, he set the brush aside. Then he took a golden razor and passed the blade across my grandfather's chin with extreme care. When the man, who had remained silent this whole time and had not looked at my face, was finished, my grandfather picked up a bottle of aftershave that he applied to his face. He wiped his face with a silk towel. Getting up, he came over and took me in his arms. I savoured the smell of his spirit and clung to it.

'How are you, my dear?' he said in a serious tone. Then he came over, sat down, and pulled me onto his lap after moving the cat aside to make room. It stood under his feet, meowing tenderly.

'I'm afraid, Grandfather.'

'Don't be afraid, my child. How is your grandmother doing, and her sons and daughters? How is our house and our garden? How are the people there?'

'Grandfather, I'm afraid. I love you, but I don't want to stay here.'

'Don't be afraid. You will leave this place. Tell me about all of you. What befell you after my departure?'

I sat with him for many hours, telling him all the details I knew about life there. He put his hand to his cheek and watched me, without showing the least surprise. When I started feeling tired, I told him, 'I have nothing else to add.'

'My dear grandchild, we in the world of the dead do not sleep well on account of the pain we suffer for our countries.

We feel a sense of failure and shame towards you for having left you in agony aboard the ship we chose for you without your wanting it.'

'Grandfather, is it true that we live aboard a ship?'

He got up from his place and took me by the hand. We went up to a small hill behind his dwelling and from there descended into a deep valley filled with flowers. After that, we stood at the edge of a vast well that opened to the centre of the planet. He threw in a flower he had plucked from a branch hanging down nearby. A few seconds later, I was surprised to see our neighbourhood appearing clearly before me. From this perspective high in the sky, it appeared just like an actual ship with its sail, tower and anchor. I recognised my school. I saw the shelter. After that, I found the Baghdad Clock, the Ma'mun Tower and the suspension bridge. Then I came across our house and cried as loudly as I could, 'I want Mama and Papa!'

'Go in peace, my granddaughter. Tell your grandmother that I'm well and that I live a blessed life. Kiss each palm and every other tree in our city for me. Kiss the river, the ground and the air there. Go, my granddaughter! You are late. Life is there, life in the birthplace that is even more beautiful than this blessed existence.'

A tear like a crystal ball sprang from his eye, and before he left, he looked into my eyes and said, 'Do you remember how many palm trees there are at our house?'

'Inside the wall, there are four palm trees, Grandpa.'

'Tell your grandmother to take care of them.'

'Yes, Grandpa, I'll tell her. But can I take the cat with me? My friend has been looking for it a long time, and she was overjoyed when she found it here.'

'No, my daughter, this is my cat, and it cheers me up. In your world, it lived blind.'

The cat jumped up on me to give me a kiss and then jumped over to Grandfather, who held it to his chest as he moved away, muttering to himself, 'Four palm trees – dear Lord! Four palm trees that I left behind at my old house and that I wish might be here.'

A little later, a swallow came and guided me towards the Nineveh gate, through which I had entered earlier. I went out and found Nadia waiting for me at the entrance to the shelter. I took her hand and we went home.

27

'I missed you.'

'I missed you more, Farouq.'

Rain began to pelt down. We sought shelter under a large tree while students jostled each other, squeezing together under the narrow arcades of our college.

'Come on,' Farouq said, as though he had something to get off his chest. 'Get your books and follow me. No arguments!'

'Where to?'

'Let's walk on the Adhamiya corniche.'

I left him there and went into the lecture hall, gathered my books, and came back to meet him. Outside the university gates, we got into his car and set off for the corniche. The gulls were circling around pieces of food that floated on the surface of the water. I remembered Nadia's bag, stolen by seagulls once in a dream.

Farouq came over, and we stood close to each other on the riverbank. The smell of his cologne distracted me. I wanted to step away and leave some space between us, but something inside prevented me from moving. I kept smelling him along with the scent of the river. In that moment, I longed to embrace him forever, to fall asleep on his chest, to kiss him on the neck twenty times. I wanted him to stroke my hair, to take me with a sudden kiss and moisten my life like a wave that did not know the meaning of drought. I wished to take his hand but then hesitated and turned away.

Was Farouq also thinking about embracing me? Was he trembling from his depths out of desire for us to melt together in an everlasting moment of passion like the flow of an eternal river? His glance moved freely over the waves as I regarded his silence. How I love you, Farouq! How can I say that so you hear it from my soul? His hands came close to mine, and our fingertips brushed together. A refreshing breeze blew from the river, and my hair streamed out behind me. The sun went down across the surface of the water. Seagulls wheeled around it like a large disc of pita bread straight from a village baker's oven.

A small gull took a piece of bread from the riverbank and circled high with it. Pursued by the larger gulls, it swooped under the iron bridge and disappeared.

'War will break out soon.'

'When?'

'Soon. Everything says that it is coming, and that it will bring disaster.'

'Are you afraid of the war?'

'I'm afraid for you. For our love. For our memories. I don't know where fate is taking us. War is not a battle between two sides with a winner and a loser. War turns life upside down and scatters everything from its place, like a wild shot far off the goal. This might be the last time we stand on this riverbank. The last time we are able to take a walk in the daylight.'

'Farouq, don't say such things! I'm afraid.'

'All of us are afraid. Even the sun is afraid.'

'What's to be done? I'm so tired of the news.'

'No one knows. The little fish in the river don't have the power to decide which way the water flows. Even the big fish can't affect its direction. We are like the little fish in this river. We don't know where the waves will cast us up.'

'Farouq, you've become so old and wise.'

'In this country, a person grows ten years in a single day.'

'I want to stay young. I don't like the idea of being in the world of adults. I want us to be young forever. You and me and Nadia and the whole neighbourhood.'

'Speaking of Nadia, what's going on with her?'

'Nadia has grown up because that's what she wants. Even I no longer know who she is. I've started fearing that she will enter the world of adults and leave me. Do you want us to go and see her now?'

'Where is she?'

'At university, in Al-Jadriya.'

'Let's go.'

Before we even made it through the university gates, we found Nadia on her way out, about to board her bus. She was delighted to see us there, and even more delighted to learn we were there to visit her. She made her excuses to the bus driver and came walking with us. The three of us headed towards the bridge and decided to wander without any fixed destination.

On the way, after a few minutes of silence, Nadia took a letter out of her bag with a photo folded inside it. Ahmad had sent it from Mosul with the sister of a female friend who studied with him in the same college. Nadia put the letter back in her bag and just gave me the photo. I understood from the way she looked at me that the photo conveyed unpleasant news.

The picture showed a group of students in the architectural department. At the right-hand end of the row, Ahmad stood smiling, his shoulder pressed against the shoulder of a blonde girl, whose features at first glance were startlingly beautiful. I passed the photo to Farouq, who held it close to examine the details more closely. He gave it one last look before handing it to me without a single word. Nadia observed our significant silence. She heaved a painful sigh and said, 'This is what I was afraid of.'

'But it's an innocent photo, Nadia.'

'If you read the letter and started making the connections between it and the picture, you'd see it's not innocent.'

'But Ahmad loves you.'

'He used to love me.'

Nadia was not alone in allowing her tears to flow freely at that moment. My own tears sought to break free for the sake of my friend as she stumbled in love. Nadia was like me. She had never before experienced emotional frustration. She did not know what it meant to change the person you loved and to cast your heart in a different direction. How was it possible for someone who loved to abandon his memories? How could he build new kingdoms of words, songs and sighs in distant cities? How could his dreams incorporate new faces? It is true that love may be born in a single moment, but it becomes established afterwards like a large city built from the soul's desire.

After wandering for an hour, Nadia felt tired. Sadness was etched on her face. We headed towards Farouq's car, and I sat with Nadia in the back. The radio was playing a song by Haitham Yousif.

Never once has my love fallen short
Never once have I done you any wrong
Your candle now lit inside me for always
My life is all lost in hard, bitter days

When we reached our street, Nadia and I got out, and the car turned and headed off in the opposite direction. From a distance, Biryad came running towards us, happy that we had come home. We stood there for several minutes petting him as he jumped up with excitement.

Before going to sleep that night, Nadia wrote Ahmad a long letter. She tore it up. She wrote a second letter and tore that one up too. She kept writing and ripping until sleep overcame her.

In her dream, she was sitting on a bench under the eucalyptus tree that they used to sit beneath in Al-Zawra, engrossed in one of her school books. She was startled by a gentle hand on her shoulder and an affectionate kiss on her cheek. Ahmad had come from behind the tree and kissed her.

There are kisses that are not what we wanted, and that we are not ready for. Kisses that do not make us melt from love, yet make us love ourselves and everything around us.

28

Uncle Shawkat took his winter coat from the cupboard and put it on over his clothes. He went into the back garden and set the nightingale free from its cage. He did the same for the partridges after putting their food in the dry irrigation canal.

Without taking a good look at himself in the mirror as he had always done throughout the many years of his life, Uncle Shawkat went out to the street, Biryad at his heels. Biryad had grown up and had taken on responsibilities. He ran on ahead of his owner to ensure the way was safe. Uncle Shawkat stopped by some of the abandoned houses, and then he headed for Abu Nabil's shop. He joined the circle of elderly neighbourhood men who always sat there in the evening. Meanwhile, the dog settled down a few steps away, watching the eyes of his owner.

Abu Hussam was greatly pained by Uncle Shawkat's insistence that he retell an old story, one he had told many times before, of something that had happened during his work as a supervisor for the railway. Abu Hussam spoke very little those days. His hours were filled with sorrow over the murder of his daughter and the flight of her brother. But he loved Uncle Shawkat and told him the story once again in a tired voice. Uncle Shawkat could not hear him clearly – he had become partially deaf – and Abu Hussam had to repeat himself over and over, raising his voice so that Uncle Shawkat might hear. It was no good.

The rest of the men felt badly that their neighbour had sunk to this state. He had been known for how he cared for his health and for the elegance of his attire, and now he went about in a down-at-heel way that did not suit him. Uncle Shawkat sensed their sympathetic glances in his direction. They contained something like pity, which he could not abide.

'I am Shawkat Ibrahim Oglu,' he said to himself, but in a voice that everyone could hear. 'I've lived an honourable life, and I will die an honourable death.' Without another word, he got up and left them, his dog walking a few steps ahead.

No one was annoyed. On the contrary, they began recalling their neighbour's attitude, his upstanding morals, and the way he had always lived by looking out for everyone in the neighbourhood. They were sad at how his life had deteriorated. Of all the men in the neighbourhood, Uncle Shawkat had been the most generous and good-hearted, just as his outer appearance had been a model of good taste.

For his own part, Uncle Shawkat guessed that the conversation would turn to him when he left the gathering. Deep down, he knew how much his neighbours loved him and valued the good relationships that had persisted for so many years.

'There's no hope for this life. All the beautiful days have passed, never to return. Ever since the first family left and emigrated far away, the neighbourhood has not been the same. At this point, there's nothing for me to do except count out the unimportant days and live them by force of habit. If it weren't for my responsibility for the abandoned houses, I would leave this place and go and spend my final years in my village near Kirkuk.'

He went inside the house and brought out a thick rug that he unrolled behind the broken-down car. He decided to sleep there that night. He was tired of sleeping in his dark room, where he felt suffocated by the walls and ceiling. He stretched out on his back, put the radio on his chest, and looked up at the stars above.

Biryad lay down nearby with a deep sadness in his eyes. The weather was mild that evening, but after midnight, a chill breeze accompanied by some light drops of rain blew over them. Uncle Shawkat carried the rug inside, stuffed it under the stairs without folding it first, and stretched out on the sofa.

Before closing his eyes, Uncle Shawkat remembered Biryad, whom he had left outside. He got up to call him, wanting Biryad to come in and sleep in the living room with him. Taking this compassionate step towards his companion relaxed the lines on his face.

The following morning, he saw the neighbours gathered at the door of Umm Rita's house. He fell to his knees and let out a hoarse cry when he discovered that the house had been robbed of everything in it. The thieves had left nothing behind except a small statue of the Holy Virgin thrown disrespectfully in the front doorway with a chain of black prayer beads wrapped around its neck.

Neighbours gathered around him, taking him in their arms in an attempt to quell his tears. But he clung to the gate and continued his lament with a broken heart. He turned to the dog and began cursing him savagely for not having fulfilled his duty. Biryad too began whimpering, and then he ran off.

That evening, Uncle Shawkat carried his mattress, his blanket, some tools and the radio to the entrance of Umm Rita's house, having decided to sleep there to guard it in case the thieves returned.

After that incident, Uncle Shawkat no longer had much confidence in the dog. He took upon himself the role of volunteer night watchman to keep watch over the houses that had been abandoned by their families. He observed from afar with suspicion the movement of strangers, blowing a whistle that Farouq gave him. He tried with all his might to protect the past from passing away.

Day after day, Uncle Shawkat's health deteriorated and his eyesight weakened. He dragged his feet along with difficulty. He never took off his heavy winter coat even in the hot afternoon hours. He forgot his habit of bathing daily, and he began going inside his house only to use the toilet or to make food or tea, which he drank from a thermos in order to keep it warm throughout the day. His own house took on a half-abandoned appearance.

Neighbours new to the area considered him crazy. But those of us who were native to the place had a different image of Uncle Shawkat rooted deeply within us: clean-shaven and wearing an elegant suit, shoes and tie, as he used his teeth to make round watches on children's wrists before giving them sweets. We believed that this condition of his was a kind of emergency like every other emergency in our lives, a momentary crisis that would certainly pass when his vigour returned.

One month before the war began, Uncle Shawkat was detained by the government on account of suspicions regarding his behaviour and the dramatic change that had come over him. The government paid close attention whenever anyone's behaviour changed, suspecting even the sick when their condition changed as the illness ran its course. They took Uncle Shawkat away without justification and without any consideration for the state of his health.

During this period, Biryad lived as though homeless. He refused invitations from the neighbours to spend the night in their houses. He no longer ate the food we put out for him; he wouldn't even approach us.

The dog deeply regretted what he considered to be his mistake, even though that was not really the case. It was

Uncle Shawkat who had invited Biryad to sleep with him in
the living room that night, and the thieves had exploited that
when they robbed Umm Rita's house.

Uncle Shawkat was released seven days later. His condition
was even more miserable than before. It was not that his
appearance was worse, but rather the sight of the president's
picture, firing a gun into the air, hanging around his neck.
Biryad was delighted at Uncle Shawkat's return and resumed
following him like his shadow.

War anthems rose in earnest. Everyone believed the war
would come any minute. Uncle Shawkat carried a wooden
extension ladder to a tall building at the end of the street.
He leaned it against the wall and climbed up with difficulty.
Using long nails, he attached a large piece of cardboard to
the front of the building that read, 'Neighbourhood for sale
or rent.'

War broke out a few days later. Bombs began falling at
dawn, and we were instantly reminded of the atmosphere in
the city in 1991. This time, however, we were used to it, so we
were less afraid. Our lives did not merit much fear. We felt a
strong desire to make it to the end, no matter what that end
might be. The bombs fell here and there, and day and night
the planes circled overhead, but we did not go to the shelter,
nor did we crouch under the stairs.

People sat outside their houses, listening to the radio for
the latest news. I would say that life felt normal. But everyone
was waiting to see what would happen next. The weather
was beautiful in those days, despite the black smoke that rose
in every direction. It was an opportunity to gather together
in the neighbourhood since the schools, universities and
offices had closed. Everyone had plenty of time to go out
to the street and mingle with others. Nadia, Baydaa and I
would meet in the garden at my house. Then we would go to

the front door to watch life, which had become so calm. How had life become calm with all these bombs and explosions? Sometimes, in tense moments, peace comes from within, and an unfamiliar assurance pervades our souls, rising up from despair, from the desire to live, or from something else that I cannot put my finger on.

Baghdad fell...

Flames erupted everywhere; smoke rose on all sides. Fire consumed the thick piece of cardboard that Uncle Shawkat had hung at the top of the street, and it crumbled into black ash in the air.

I fled with my family to my grandmother's house in the country, far from Baghdad. There, I lived several months of relative peace far from the chaos that had befallen everything. I adapted to the life of nature with the birds and the murmuring water in the canals. My features relaxed, just as my clothes changed, along with my way of sleeping, eating and drinking. Everything in my life changed.

When the sun went down, I missed Nadia, Baydaa, Farouq, our house and our neighbourhood. I would sit alone on the riverbank, close to the waterwheels, watching the small waves push the fishermen's boats towards the bridge.

Years before, I had been a small child when I came here to escape the old war, and now, here I was again, having fled this new one. The same planes and the same bombs drove me away after twelve years of sanctions.

What had Bush the Father wanted from my life? And what was it that Bush the Son sought from it?

How would I tell these stories to my children in the future? How would their grandchildren believe that two presidents of a great nation had pursued my life with rockets?

But on the other hand, I ought to thank them. But for them, I would not have visited my grandmother's quieter city, this magical paradise that slumbered beside the Euphrates, this place filled with the graves and spirits of my ancestors.

My grandmother was no longer as healthy or as mobile as she had once been. The days had taken their toll, and she had started leaning against the walls as she walked. She no longer slept in her old room, where the stars shone through the windows.

At night, I stayed up with her and begged her to tell me stories. I wanted to be young again and in her lap. I wanted her to tell me once more that she was my mother: 'I gave birth to you from this tummy before I bore your mother.'

My grandmother smiled at me as she struggled against the pains in her body. As I looked into her tired face, I was thinking that she would one day leave this life, and our relationship would be ended, once and for all, in this place that protected me from wars.

This merciful spot of earth was not a ship at anchor, waiting for the sign to embark. This was truly a piece of ground attached to its memory, close to its original nature. Even the palm trees here were the descendants of trees that had rooted in this place for thousands of years. The birds here did not build new nests for their young, but restored old nests to settle in. The fish here resisted the flow of the river, using tricks in order to stay in place and play with the waterwheels.

I kissed the palm trees, I kissed the ground and the water, I kissed the air and I kissed everything that my grandfather loved. I went into my grandmother's dark room and looked at his picture, which used to protect me from thieves.

'I've kissed everything that you asked me to, Grandfather. Do you want anything else from me?'

Grandfather smiled at me from the picture. He lifted his cap off his head and set it aside.

I remembered his home in the City of Light. I remembered the scent of the paradise he lived in. I remembered his love for the land, and a tear fell from my eye.

That night, I sat with my grandmother, kissed her forehead, gave her a hug, and went to sleep beside her. The following day we would return to Baghdad. Things had deteriorated, and there was no hope that the situation would stabilise. 'There's nothing to do but accept reality and adapt to it,' my father repeated, my mother nodding her head.

I got up in the morning and made breakfast for my grandmother. It was like the ones she used to make for me in my childhood. We ate together without a single word. I kissed her hand and then got up, taking my bag.

We returned to our house in Baghdad. We all helped clean it and sweep away the dust that had piled up everywhere. We reinforced the locks on the windows and doors with thick iron chains. Then we fell asleep, exhausted.

Our spacious, comfortable house, with its clean air, where the sun circled and shone in from every side, had become dark and depressed. Strange ghosts moved across its roof. The comfort of a house comes from the comfort of its people, and our house was not happy in those days. Pervaded by dreariness, it breathed polluted air and choked on its own tears. Have you seen houses cry? I often heard the walls of our house groaning. I saw its tears with my own eyes and cried along with it.

I was born in this house, and in it I uttered my first sounds. I spoke my first 'papa' and my first 'mama'. On these tiles I learned to stand and take a step. I fell down, got up, and took another step. When I walked towards the door for the first time, the light of the world was revealed to me, and through that door the wars entered. In this house I saw things as they were in their reality. I saw the door as a door, the street as a street, the window as a window. I saw the tree as a tree and the rose as a rose. Where did that old clarity go, which solid things used to offer? Why did the door lose the power of its existence, the tree its presence, the flower its touch? In childhood, we see things as they are in all their clarity. We live as real things in direct contact. We feel them and become aware of the power of their outpouring in front of us. Why do these things change and become strange and confused, losing their substance?

Door, window, house, tree, dog, cat, sparrow, stove, chair, rack: when we say things separately, we feel the weight of their soul. When we put them in complete sentences, we kill that soul. Why did we learn to speak of things in complete sentences? Things in themselves are complete without sentences.

In those days devoid of meaning, I came across the novel *One Hundred Years of Solitude* in my father's library. Through it, I travelled from our neighbourhood to the village of Macondo, whose people were afflicted with the same insomnia that we were living through. We too no longer took any pleasure in sleeping. Forgetfulness began erasing the blackboard of our collective memory. We would pass by Uncle Shawkat, and it was as though we did not know him like we used to. We would pass by houses and forget the names of their inhabitants. The forms of things changed, and a single thing would come to possess many names. Language was no longer blessed with good health. Liberation, fall, occupation, invasion, destruction: how could all these words apply to a single day?

Days that do not have a clear name – those are the days when hope ends. Limp days without sufficient strength to face the future.

The contagion of multiple names was transferred to the people themselves. A name began referring not to an individual person but rather to his religious affiliation. A large number of young men lived difficult days with more than one name and address. When you renounce your name, how will you know other people?

Only Farouq was unable to change his name since he was a famous football player who everyone knew. He came one day in the early afternoon. Summoning his courage, he knocked on the door of our house. When no one answered, he slid into our garage a short letter telling me goodbye and saying he would be leaving for Jordan in an hour. My mother stumbled across the letter and picked it up with a trembling hand. She thought it might be one of those letters threatening people and warning them to leave their homes. She read it quickly, and her fear subsided. Instead of tearing it up as might be expected, she came to me in the living room and threw the paper in my face without uttering a single word. I took the letter and went up to my room where I read it and cried.

My dearest beloved,

I have to travel with the youth national team. I had wanted to see you at this sad hour. Didn't I tell you the war would deprive us of the most beautiful things? Do you remember that, when we watched the sun setting over the Tigris?

I love you,

Farouq

Two days later, I asked my mother to take me to Nadia's house. I missed her, and I wanted to cry on her shoulder. My mother opened our gate and looked out with fearful eyes, examining the street carefully to the right and left. When she saw Biryad walking around and wagging his white tail, she was sure the area was free of strangers. She put an abaya over my head. It was the first time I had worn one, and this one was actually my mother's.

We walked quickly to Nadia's house. Her brother, Muayad, was sitting on an old chair at the gate and got up to greet us. My mother returned home, while I entered the house without knocking and walked straight into the front room, just like I used to do as a child. Startled, Nadia leaped from her seat, and with an astonishment as great as a city's when suddenly captured, she wrapped her arms around my neck. That was the first time we had met since Baghdad had fallen.

We went up to her room, and my tears flowed down onto her shoulder. She cried with me, and I stayed with her until sunset. Then I returned to my house escorted by Muayad, who made sure I arrived safely before saying goodbye and returning home.

Visiting Nadia's house became a daily habit for me in that slow time. I would put an abaya over my head and go to see her. I stopped the day an American soldier on patrol through our neighbourhood catcalled me. Nadia became the one to visit me on a daily basis, her brother accompanying her all the way to our gate. Sometimes she would spend the night with me, and we would stay up till sunrise before going to sleep.

I lent her García Márquez's novel. She returned it to me the next day, saying, 'It's long, and the names are complicated. I didn't understand a thing.'

As for me, I reread the novel more than once. It formed for me a magical, parallel world that allowed me to escape the pressure of the difficult days that our neighbourhood was living through.

The Americans detained Nadia's father. They came back the next day and detained her brother. After several days, they released her father, while her brother was kept for more than a week before they set him free through the intervention of Marwa, who had begun working as a translator with the American army. To protect their lives, her family had been forced to leave their home and go into hiding.

29

One day in July during the first year of the occupation, Marwa visited us, disguised in an abaya and large sunglasses. Speaking in a low voice and looking left and right to give extra weight to her words, she said, 'The Americans suspect that groups of militants are hiding in the abandoned houses. Some Marine units will come tomorrow to surround the area and search the houses one by one. They will conduct night-time raids on everyone.' She went on to advise us to cooperate, since they had clear instructions to open fire on anyone they suspected.

Before leaving, Marwa told us in a whisper, as though she were divulging a dangerous secret, 'They are searching for Ahmad.'

My eyes followed her as she walked away from the alley. I remembered the flag-raising ceremonies and the bullets from her rifle that would startle the sparrows out of their nests. But despite all that, I loved her. I loved something inside her, there in the depths of her soul. There was another Marwa that resembled our childhood. Even though she had been speaking with my parents without looking at me, I kept my gaze focused on her face, looking for her old eyes, for her nose, for the shape of the mouth she had used as a child to pick on us in the street. We had grown up in the same place, breathed the same air. We had played here on the pavement of this street, under the light of this street lamp.

'They're searching for Ahmad.'

It is your young heart, Marwa, that was searching for Ahmad. When we lived through our teenage years, you tried to catch him with songs and smiles, but he loved Nadia. And now you come with the greatest military power in history to catch him again. What a passionate lover you are, Marwa! How stubborn and strong you are! But that's life, Marwa, and that's love. You cannot compel it with force, even with the greatest military power in history. Love comes from a different place. All the technology of the Marines is incapable of finding it out, but the heart of a young woman in love knows it well. You are beautiful and smart, and a thousand Ahmads desire you. Let love come and knock on the door of your heart, unlooked for. Do not drive it away with planes, armoured cars and bullets. Leave Ahmad alone! Let him live how he wants at a time when even the oxygen in the air is deadly poison.

Before leaving the neighbourhood for the last time, Marwa stopped at the door of Umm Rita's house to greet Uncle Shawkat. She went up and greeted him eloquently and respectfully. She tried to remind him of her name, of his teeth marks on her wrist, but to no avail. She slipped a small amount of cash into his pocket. A tear fell from her eye, and she took out her handkerchief to wipe it away.

When Uncle Shawkat used to bite our wrists in the days when we were young, he did not know that we would grow up this quickly. He had wanted us to remain children who wore our imaginary watches, pressed by his teeth into our delicate skin. He knew that it hurt us a little to bite our tender wrists, but it was a pain that caused pleasure for both parties, a pleasure we felt without being able to preserve it. Those hours effaced by time kept circling within our depths, drawing zigzag lines between our childhood and our future. The Marines came for our future and smashed its windows.

They demolished everything. They destroyed the lives of us children who grew up in this place. Their tanks wiped the traces of our childhood from the streets.

Why are there no longer any children in our street to offer their wrists to Uncle Shawkat for him to make watches? These days, it was his own lips he would bite, a practice that could express any number of things. Indeed, gnawing on his lips had become Uncle Shawkat's sole language with everyone. There was one bite for memory and another for pain, a gentle bite when he met someone he loved, and a snap at the air when he passed a house that had belonged to neighbours who had departed, a powerful bite that planted the upper teeth into his lower lip. It was when he saw an American tank breaking up the street's pavement and wiping away the familiar steps that had been imprinted there for twenty years that he lost the power to speak and developed this habit of biting his lips.

Uncle Shawkat got up the following morning and, dragging himself along heavily, set off to knock on Umm Ahmad's door. She went out and tried, without success, to understand the meaning of the rapid bites on his lower lip. She called her son. Ahmad had been listening to the news on the radio, and he stood before Uncle Shawkat, who went to him, took hold of his left hand, and bent over to press into his wrist the deep imprint of a watch, something he had forgotten he used to do when Ahmad was a child. His glances conveyed many things he wanted to say but could not find the words to convey. Uncle Shawkat drew Ahmad's hand in a second time and waved it in space as though to say, 'Goodbye.'

Ahmad grasped the meaning of this sign, which his mother had been incapable of understanding. Uncle Shawkat went off, and Ahmad stood there, explaining the situation to his mother. She went inside and gathered their things. She soon came back, turned the key in the lock, and departed quickly with her son before anyone noticed.

The Americans came at dusk. Once they had surrounded the area, they began to raid the houses. They conducted a search, house by house, room by room, going up to the rooftops of the dwellings and digging through their gardens. Using heavy hammers, they broke the lock on the door of Umm Ahmad's house. One group went inside while another lined both sides of the street. They made a careful inspection of the rooms and then left. Was Marwa with them? Did she translate for them Nadia's letters, which Ahmad had hidden in a drawer of his desk? What did they find inside the house apart from secret love letters?

At the top of the street, we heard the sound of the first improvised explosive device exploding against an American armoured car. The battle of the IEDs had begun.

At midnight, unknown persons distributed flyers announcing, in the name of the resistance, the destruction of an American Humvee. The flyers threatened the families of those cooperating with the enemy. Life had become deeply uncertain.

Night and day, planes circled in the sky over the neighbourhood, and explosives were planted in the street.

Slogans criticising the occupation and threatening collaborators with death were written on the walls of houses, schools and government buildings everywhere. The front door of Marwa's family was painted black, with the picture of a bullet over the words 'Death to traitors'.

30

Umm Farouq left her house and made certain to lock the door. She did not inform us where she was going. In our street, none of the houses retained their original inhabitants except ours, Nadia's and Baydaa's, in addition to Uncle Shawkat's, if we wanted to count it, though in reality it was also abandoned, for the owner had not lived in it since Umm Rita's house was robbed.

The three remaining families took turns caring for Uncle Shawkat, providing him with food, tea and other necessities. Sometimes we obtained medicine for him, but he would throw it away when we were not looking. His illness was not the kind that needed a doctor's prescription: he was wounded deep in his soul by an injury the size of a giant ship that had anchored here for many years.

In those lonely days, Nadia and I began spending the night at each other's house. Each night, we would sleep together in one of our two houses and would be together nearly twenty-four hours a day. In that way, we reclaimed something of our small share of happiness.

Oh, for that happiness that can be invented even during hard times! Do I speak the truth about happiness? What was its form? What did it taste like? Was it a true happiness that people could talk about without feeling sick?

Whenever the electricity was cut during the daytime, we would sit in the garden until evening; sometimes we would do that even when the power came back. One sunny day, as we chatted on a small bench off to one side that offered a view of their whole garden, I happened to notice a piece of clear glass reflecting the flashing rays of the sun. It was tucked away among the jasmine that formed a green rectangle around the grass of the garden. I went over, picked it up, and discovered it was a half-empty bottle of liquor. It later came out that the bottle belonged to Nadia's brother, Muayad, who had hidden it there out of fear that his consuming alcohol at this early stage of his life would be found out – at a time when doing forbidden things meant death by a single bullet.

When Muayad came back to look for it, Nadia and I bargained with him, saying we would return the bottle to him on the condition that he hand over his cassette recorder. He agreed, laughing at the way we fleeced him. From then on, we had a way to listen to music.

Every morning, we would eat our breakfast listening to the songs of Fairuz. The day would continue with Kathem Al-Saher, Hatem Al-Iraqi, Mohannad Mohsen, Haitham Yousif, Raid George, and a single tape by Najat Al Saghira, which had a rasp that prevented us from hearing it well. We also found some tapes of foreign music in Nadia's mother's wardrobe: Jane Birkin, Madonna and the Beatles.

Among all these tapes, there were certain songs that spoke directly to Nadia's heart: 'Be Safe in God's Hand', 'If Only We Never Met', 'Loving You and Losing All'. When these songs played, Nadia would lose herself in dancing and forget everything – herself, Kathem's voice, even the air. I would watch, clapping enthusiastically, and then the song would end. She would wipe away her tears, sit down absent-mindedly, and recall old memories. Ahmad had abandoned her, but she loved him from the bottom of her heart. She invented one excuse after another for him: 'His circumstances in exile have pushed him to the heart of another girl, a blonde girl from Mosul. She enchanted him with her charming stutter, the force of her personality and her bewitching smile, but he'll come back.'

'He'll come back,' we would always tell ourselves, for we did not want to surrender. We did not want to transform our first stories into mere memories that lost their usefulness and were forgotten, just as our neighbourhood had forgotten its past and hung suspended in space.

In García Márquez's novel, the village of Macondo was forced to confront forgetfulness through writing. On each thing, they recorded its particular name so that forgetfulness would not wipe those names away.

Later on, the people of the village realised that their method was not sufficient, for they might know things by writing down their names, but how would they know the advantages of those things and how to use them? So they added explanations. In this way, they hung a label round the neck of the cow that would remind them to milk it and then to use that milk in their coffee.

In this way, writing does the work of protecting memory. Through it, we remember the names of things, some of their functions and how to use them. But this ignores their spiritual history. Living memory was the only thing that could protect us from the curse of the unknown.

If they had written just the word 'cow' without any clari-fication, it is possible that after the disease of forgetfulness came, they would have discovered the whole thing all over again. They would have learned how to milk the cow, one of them would have mixed the milk into his coffee, and in this way, they would have made coffee with milk, a new flavour that no one had ever tasted before. They ruined everything by writing sentences.

To combat forgetfulness in our neighbourhood as well, Nadia and I thought about writing descriptions of things. We began this experiment with ourselves. In a blue notebook we found in my father's library, we wrote: 'This is my friend Nadia. Her eyes are green, and her hair is blonde. I'm a little taller than her. I met her in a concrete air-raid shelter. That was in the year 1991. We went to primary school, middle school and secondary school together. Now she studies at the University of Baghdad and I study at the University of Technology. She loves Ahmad and I love Farouq.'

When the first pages were filled with writing about obvious things, it resembled the reading book in our first year at school: house, floor, fire and so on.

One morning we went out and wrote on the houses the names of their old inhabitants, the dates they left their homes, and the countries they now lived in. Then we transferred those details into the notebook. On the wall of Uncle Shawkat's house, for example, we wrote: 'This is Uncle Shawkat's house. His wife, Baji Nadira, left for Kurdistan after the first Gulf War in 1991. He currently lives in Umm Rita's house, and has done ever since thieves still at large stole their furniture.'

Our idea developed, and we decided to write in the same notebook twenty pages about each family in the neighbourhood to summarise their lives and our memories of them. This was the first time that our personal history as neighbours had been recorded, just as our memory was at risk of passing away.

'But what is the name of this record?' Nadia asked me.

'*The Baghdad Clock.*'

'No. Let's name it *The Record of a Neighbourhood.*'

'*The Baghdad Clock: The Record of a Neighbourhood*,' I replied without too much thought and without knowing why this name occurred to me. Nadia agreed immediately, and on the cover of the notebook, we wrote in big letters: *The Baghdad Clock: The Record of a Neighbourhood*.

Here is a sample from the notebook:

The house with the wide black gate is the house of Umm Ali. The house that the red car goes into is the house of Umm Manaf. Umm Hussam's house is the one whose grape vines hang down over ours. The house with ivy creeping up and covering its windows is Umm Wijdan's. The house that Devil Girl plays in front of is the house of Umm Osama. The house where the daughter got married and many colourful cars came to take her away with music is the house of Umm Salli. The house where we go to sing at New Year is the house of Umm Rita. Next door is the house of Umm Marwan, and after that is the house of Umm Ahmad. Then the house of Umm Baydaa, and after it the house of Umm Farouq. Last is the house of Uncle Shawkat, and Abu Nabil's shop.

Taking Umm Salli's house as an example, they are a family composed of a mother, a father and five daughters, all of whom are remarkably beautiful. Umm Salli never gave birth to a son, and she often recounts how she dreamed on her wedding night that she would be deprived of sons, but that God would compensate her with beautiful daughters, all of whom would marry foreigners and live in distant cities.

Take Sahir, for example. She is the fourth of Umm Salli's five daughters, and when she left the neighbourhood with her family to go abroad, she was a captivating young woman with amber eyes and jet-black hair, rosy, dimpled cheeks, a wide forehead, a charming lisp when she spoke, and eyebrows that looked like slender spears. She was the most alluring of her sisters, and the most conscious of how to exploit her beauty in life.

She always said, 'I'll only marry a handsome pilot.' In order to fulfil this desire, Amjad, the younger son of Umm Ali, enrolled in the Air Force College so that he might achieve his wish of marrying her. He did in fact become a pilot, but by this time, she was already living in Denmark, far from her homeland, and had abandoned all her old desires. Amjad wrote to her many times, but he did not receive a single response. The last letter he wrote her was the day before his plane went down, and no trace of him has been found up until the time of this writing.

I lent García Márquez's novel to Nadia again and urged her with all my heart to read it. She returned it to me two days later, saying, 'Disturbing. Depressing.'

My father did not have anything by García Márquez in our library apart from *One Hundred Years of Solitude*, and it was most likely the only novel we had at all. I read it many times, as I have said. I had not heard of García Márquez before and I used to believe this novel was the first and last written by a magical novelist who lived in a distant century.

One Hundred Years of Solitude is a novel written against both forgetfulness and memory at the same time. It sets forth a new world we did not know, as though it were a spiritual prescription for escaping misery. It did in fact save us from the actual conditions in Baghdad in 2003 by transforming me into an honorary citizen of the village of Macondo, where I was bound by strong ties to all the inhabitants of the village, even as I developed passing friendships with their gypsy visitors and the residents of the neighbouring swamps.

When I resumed my academic life, I secretly chose new names for my university professors that were borrowed from the inhabitants of García Márquez's village: José Arcadio Buendía, Dr Aureliano, Dr Amaranta, Professor Aureliano José, Professor Úrsula, Dr Aureliano II, Dr Rebeca.

When Nadia returned the novel to me the second time, a folded upper page corner made it clear she had stopped reading at page 59. The events of these relatively few pages out of the big novel – which was longer than 500 pages – formed the core of her dreams' narratives till the end of 2003.

Each time, her dream began with a cinematic shot at dawn in which the camera pans round, filming twenty mud-and-reed houses erected on the bank of a clear-water river. Her dream would end with José Arcadio Buendía explaining everything he knew about insomnia to the village elders.

That scene occupied my memory for a long time, and I may have been mistaken about whether it came from one of Nadia's dreams or whether it was actually produced by García Márquez's mind. Sometimes it even occurred to me that I should consider it a scene invented by my own imagination.

31

This time, I will think about the American pilot as he hovers at dawn in his Apache helicopter in the sky above Baghdad. He often flies over our neighbourhood and circles several times low over our rooftops.

I will suppose he comes from Los Angeles, or from New York, the same city where the towers fell and for which – by some illogical reasoning – we were paying the price. I will suppose that he comes from any American state, for that does not interest me personally.

He will be thinking about his wife and children whenever his eyes pass over the figure of a slender woman or a skinny child walking down the street. He will remember their home far away when he observes the roofs of our houses with their clothes lines, iron water tanks and iron bedframes waiting there for another summer.

He will think about the clean skies over his city when our dust prevents him from seeing things clearly. He will certainly think of all that. He will keep watch on the movement of the people, the cars and all the strange things moving on the ground as he passes his reports on to the command centre: 'Nothing happening here that resembles a ship. It's calm and the traffic is normal. Nothing exciting.'

Someone from the operations centre will respond: 'Sweep the area well, and photograph it from every angle in high definition. It's likely that the target is hiding in one of the neighbourhood's abandoned houses.'

The pilot circles again, moving slowly along all four sides of the neighbourhood. He stops there in the sky like an eagle eyeing its target, waiting for the right moment to strike. He photographs us one by one and then sweeps off to the east, leaving behind the sound of his helicopter's rotors ringing in our air.

I will imagine an advanced piece of equipment, the kind we believe America is able to invent. Let us suppose it is a giant device that photographs the movement of time in a given place. That location's distant past appears slowly and moves across an enormous screen the size of the sky over our city. On this screen, we see a film of our neighbourhood in black and white.

The film starts when the first brick was laid in this place, running through to the hour in which the pilot circled and went back to his base.

I sit in front of this screen to watch the past that prepared for my birth in this street. That sweet childhood, jumping through hopscotch squares. Please, be so good as to watch with me! Here is the first wedding celebration in our side street. Here I am at age two. My young mother is holding me as she follows the sound of traditional music coming from Umm Nabil's house. Their daughter Amira has got married, and people are coming with a new car decorated with colourful ribbons and a big bouquet of flowers to take the bride far from the neighbourhood. They take her away amid a carnival of colours created by the radiant clothes of the beautiful girls dancing in front of the bridal car.

Look! See the young men in army uniforms, heading off before dawn for distant military bases along the border where the Iraq–Iran war is taking place. These young men… Hear their heavy boots striking the night-time asphalt.

This is the propane vendor, and this the vegetable man, circling with his cart from one alley to the next. Here are children wearing small backpacks and heading off to school.

There is the country's flag over a rented car. It is Adil, the first martyr that the war sent home to us in a wooden coffin. Listen with me to the tears: they belong to his wife, Umm Ahmad, as she mourns him with tears that will never end.

This is the fire in Umm Ali's house: a gas canister explodes in their house, and the neighbours all rush out to extinguish the fire and save the house. This small garden belongs to Umm Rita's house. There is her husband sitting under the orange tree behind a table with some meze and a bottle of beer. Here is Umm Nizar sitting in her doorway all day long, draped in black. She is waiting for her only son, whom she beseeches heaven to send back safely from the war.

This is Abu Nabil's shop, and these children are us as we make our way there. These young men are the first football team from our neighbourhood, and these old cans in the middle of the street form the goal they strive to hit. That young woman on the rooftop is Najat, and that young man making signs to her from the roof of the neighbouring house is Ali. The rainbow between them is a story of secret love that joins their hearts.

There are many things I can see on the American pilot's screen, things that, to be perfectly accurate, exist in my head, in my memory. Small scenes, nonsensical stories, overlapping voices – I can summon them up before me now. All these things form my relationship to this place.

This is where I myself was born and where my personality crystallised. In this place, my spirit grew like a tree with no history. Right here, in this square that the pilot photographs from all four sides, I became that idea dropped into time.

I was little when Baydaa's grandfather died. That may have been the first time in my life that a question about the meaning of our existence occurred to me. Where do people go after they die?

Why do we exist in the first place?

Death is a collective attention to the voice of Abdul Basit Abdul Samad as he recites *alif lam mim* at the beginning of a sura from the Qur'an. His heavenly voice draws a straight, sharp line between our existence in this world and the eternal unknown.

What the American pilot does not know is that this place is the first planet I settled on when arriving out of non-existence, and I established my personal civilisation here. In this place, I have slept more than 7,300 nights, have woken more than 7,300 times, and have heard my name repeated more than 7,300 million times.

Dear pilot, be so good as not to hover over the past! You photograph my steps in the road, count my breaths in the air, and make it difficult for my shadow to observe its habit of following me.

When the sun sets over our neighbourhood, the night becomes responsible for guarding our shadows, which the daytime laid down upon the pavements: our zigzagging shadows, our straight shadows, squat or stretched, our ghostly shadows cast by street lamps in the night.

Even those who have left us – traces of their shadows walk on the walls after we sleep. This neighbourhood is a planet of sad shadows. I beg you not to harm them.

When you land your helicopter close to the edge of our houses, it shakes the dust of our souls. Sparrows and doves are startled into flight; the blankets on our beds billow into the air. Memories bolt, gasping for the sky that is our neighbourhood's share of mercy.

Dear pilot, be merciful with us! Do not harm this sky that we have raised with dreams, prayers, sighs, laughter, songs and mothers' laments.

32

One early afternoon, Nadia, Baydaa and I were in my garden, killing time and listening to songs on the new tapes Baydaa brought from home. At a certain point, we heard a car stop outside Uncle Shawkat's house and Biryad's fierce bark. Curiosity prompted us to watch what was happening through the wide gaps in the gate.

The driver got out, wearing traditional Kurdish dress. He began knocking on the door while the dog dug at the ground with his left paw some distance away. When no one answered, a tall, slender woman got out of the car. She wore magnificent clothes and had a translucent red shawl over her head. When the dog saw her, he stopped barking as though he knew her from before.

We did not recognise her at first, but when her face turned towards us, we shouted, 'Baji Nadira!' We opened the gate and went out to welcome her joyfully.

Baji Nadira was a sudden breeze wafting over our souls from the past, from our childhood. She pulled us to her breast as she asked our names in order to recognise us and remember. From her towering height, she stroked us and leaned over to kiss our heads tenderly, time after time. Her tenderness and her kisses, which we had missed for such a long time, touched our souls once again.

'You're all grown up, my daughters.'

Baydaa summarised Uncle Shawkat's story for her. Baji told the driver to wait at the door of the house, and she hurried with us towards Umm Rita's house. Biryad – who seemed delighted at her arrival even though he had never seen her in his life – got there before us.

Baji's husband was sitting on an old chair at the edge of the garden with his long beard and baggy clothes, rocking from side to side. Baji was stunned by the unexpected appearance of the companion of her life story, the most elegant, vigorous and self-confident man she had known. She let out a suppressed cry and rushed forward to embrace him. For his part, he looked at her with a gaze old enough to encompass three lifetimes. She began raining hot kisses on his face, his hand, his foot, as her hands passed over his face to confirm what her eyes were telling her, that this sad scene was not a figment of her imagination.

Baji touched his forehead with a palm filled with the longing of the years. She tried to raise him from his seat to bring him home. Uncle Shawkat was biting hard on his lips as he gripped the chair with a child's stubbornness. Baji sat down at his feet, crying bitterly. She kept him company with Kurdish words loaded with sorrow, bitterness and longing.

Biryad was nodding his head with each word she said, just as if he understood their meaning. At each word, he also shed a tear that hung suspended on his whiskers before falling to the ground.

Some curious people tried to gather in the courtyard, but Biryad barked them away. Nadia hurried to the gate to glare at them. This was a family matter, private to the neighbourhood and its history, and not within the rights of strangers to disturb.

After a while, my parents and Nadia's joined us. Baji Nadira wept as she pulled them to her breast, exchanging tears with them that resembled little rocks rolling down a barren mountain, tears the likes of which the history of sadness in this place had never seen.

My father went up to Uncle Shawkat slowly and whispered some words in his ear. At that, Uncle Shawkat released his grip on the chair, sat up and became more relaxed. My father took him gently by the hand and led him towards our house. Baydaa's parents joined us afterwards.

In our garden, that hour saw the last gathering of the remnants of the neighbourhood. My mother wasted no time in preparing lunch, and I brought a tray of food to the Kurdish driver, who was waiting for Baji outside her house.

Lunch ended and we drank tea. My father whispered a second time in the ear of Uncle Shawkat, who had remained still for a long time. Uncle Shawkat got up and put his hand in the hand of his wife, who was exhausted by her tears. The two of them went towards their abandoned house, walking with those familiar steps that we all knew so well, steps we preserved deep in our hearts. They went inside as the dog waited at the door, keeping watch over the driver.

Before evening fell, Uncle Shawkat emerged on the street in all his elegance. Biryad followed him with silent sorrow, a gleaming tear burning in each eye. Uncle Shawkat had shaved off his beard and his thick moustache and had combed his hair into its former style. He had also reclaimed his power of speech, but in the Turkoman language this time. He had come to bid us farewell. In her limited Arabic, Baji Nadira translated his affectionate feelings towards the neighbours of his life, along with his gratitude towards them for their kindness to him throughout the time he had lived among them.

Uncle Shawkat took out of his pocket an old photo belonging to Umm Salli's house. He kissed it seven times and handed it to me. He gave his dog a deep look without a single word, tears streaming from his eyes. With a gesture of his hand, he told the dog to stay. Biryad sat there, looking at his owner in a way that broke our hearts. It was the first time we had seen him submissive and quiet, acquiescing to fate.

Uncle Shawkat returned to his house and wrote on its door in Turkoman: 'This house not for sale or rent.' He got into the car with his wife, and the two of them departed.

Biryad remained in his place, twisting his neck from side to side, not believing what had just happened. I sat beside him, petting his head and shoulders, but he did not move from that spot. Everyone gathered around, watching him in silence as though he were a pile of sadness.

Biryad lifted his gaze to the sky where the dejected purple sunset streamed down. He got up and paced heavily to the end of the street, where he looked in the direction that the car had taken. He came back to our gate, his eyes beseeching us not to abandon him too. We brought him inside. He stretched out in the garden and slept for three days straight.

Thus, our neighbourhood was opened up to interlopers, and our empty houses became free for the taking. Uncle Shawkat, who had guarded the cemetery of the unknown, had left us. We faced life without memories floating over us from a past we had shared, laugh by laugh, tear by tear. That first night passed like one of the longest nights in history. After Uncle Shawkat's departure, in the very moment that Baji Nadira's car had turned the corner and we lost sight of it, we were certain that our appointment with eternal exile had begun. Our ship was about to sound the siren to embark.

Without Uncle Shawkat, this depressing place could no longer claim to be a neighbourhood. When Baji and her driver came, they stole the past from under our feet, and we tumbled into a well of forgetfulness. Were it not for *The Baghdad Clock: The Record of a Neighbourhood*, which we wrote with the pen of memory, the neighbourhood and all its history would have been merely a long winter night's dream that we forgot in the morning.

Some days later, strangers moved into Umm Rita's house and threw the statue of the Virgin into the street. They renovated the place, painted its walls with bright colours, and wrote over the front door, 'By the grace of our Lord'.

The Lord had granted them a big house with a beautiful garden. This Lord, who had shown favour upon them with such a great blessing, certainly was not the same Lord to whom Umm Rita had prayed, lighting candles to seek forgiveness and mercy. He was not the same Lord whom my grandmother beseeched to protect us from the bombs, nor the same Lord whom Umm Ali invoked every evening in the courtyard of their house. Any Lord, who, by his grace, had granted them a house that was fully furnished, even with its stock of memories, but for which they did not lay a single brick – he could only be Satan himself.

In that big house which the Lord had bestowed upon strangers, we would gather every New Year's Eve to celebrate with a Christmas tree lit up in the far corner of the living room. Under a picture of the Virgin and her swaddling infant, prayers, praise, anthems and hymns would be lifted up. We would gather there, waiting for gifts from Papa Noël, our pockets filled with sweets. Then we would go out into the cold of our street, singing songs and walking by the light of lanterns lit by slender candles.

New years were born in that place. In that corner, right there in Umm Rita's house, the new year drew its first breath. The years are born as children, and then they grow.

Were the years growing? Or were they just piling up in this house, settling forever in that clear space called the past? How is the past unknown when we know it as well as we know our own names?

We do not remember the future. Essentially, life is a past moving forward behind us as we hurry on ahead. As for the future, it is the house of non-existence.

On the last night before Uncle Shawkat's departure, Nadia dreamed of the last chapter in García Márquez's novel – how, on the night of the festival, Pilar Ternera died in her rocking chair, and how her final wishes were honoured when she was buried not in a coffin, but rather sitting on her chair, lowered on fibre ropes by eight men into a giant grave.

33

Baydaa brought a small bag of clothes and other things and came to sleep at our house. Nadia had persuaded her with the idea that we three would stay up together that sad night following Uncle Shawkat's departure. On the table in my room, Baydaa came across the blue notebook with *The Baghdad Clock: The Record of a Neighbourhood* written on the cover. She began to flip through its pages with such great interest – passion, even – that she forgot we were there with her in the room.

Baydaa was surprised by this crazy idea. She had put her finger in the middle of the notebook and looked us in the face without uttering a single word. Then she opened it up again and read, page by page, line by line, word by word.

Without asking our permission, she took a black pen from my table and began to write without stopping, as though she were drinking the words from a pouring rain cloud of memory. She wrote everything she knew and remembered about houses, people, events and special occasions. She remembered the kinds of cars in the neighbourhood, their owners and the date they first came down our street. She recorded a summary of the cats, the dogs, the birds and the butterflies which found themselves there. She listed the palm trees, the fruit trees and the plants, indicating how old they were, how tall they were and where they were situated. She listed the flowers and the gardens they grew in. She made a map of the street lamps and the telephone poles. She enumerated the water tanks on the roofs and how large they were. She compiled a list of the most delicious foods we were used to eating and the women who were famous for each dish. She drew a chart for professions and jobs that each family member in the neighbourhood held and a chart for the school stage of each individual in the household. She noted the births, recent and old, along with the dates, the names of each child, and details about their appearance. She mentioned the names of the living grandmothers and grand-fathers in each family. She remembered the marriages, people falling in love, engagements and divorces that the neighbour-hood's families had seen in their day. She made a list of the most handsome young men and the most beautiful young women. She summarised the famous people who had come from our neighbourhood. She detailed the names of shops and stores, along with who owned them. She described the furniture of the houses she had been in throughout her life: the colour of the curtains and the kinds of rugs and carpets. She listed the names of the women who ran each household, along with their nicknames in the neighbourhood.

Baydaa named the families she believed to be the happiest or the kindest; likewise, the ones that felt the deepest misery. She wrote an account of the temperament of each person she knew well: their taste in clothes and appearance and the songs they usually listened to. She unearthed details that had been forgotten along the way. She organised a list of the words most commonly used in the neighbourhood's lexicon. She made a separate page for proverbs and popular jokes, going back and forth between each category and treating their histories and the circumstances or the difficult situations in which they would be cited. She classified the children's games and when they appeared and disappeared, discussing the most skilful player in each game.

Baydaa stayed up almost till dawn. She kept writing and writing without ever tiring of it. Sleep overcame Nadia and me, and we left Baydaa absorbed in her writing, just as though she were answering the questions in an exam with details she had learned by heart. When we awoke in the morning, Baydaa had surrendered to sleep. Nadia told me her dream about García Márquez's novel, and before she finished I smiled to remind her that I had seen it too.

Baydaa slept all morning, the notebook open beside her pillow. The black pen was still fixed between her fingers as though she had not yet finished her task.

We gently pulled the notebook away and began flipping through her pages. We were dazzled by the wealth of information she had recorded from her prodigious memory, which did not leave out anything related to our neighbourhood, even as she avoided recording any boring details. In that way, we had a memory that was nearly complete. The full history was now in our hands. In *The Baghdad Clock: The Record of a Neighbourhood*, all that beautiful time slept. Its pages contained a living memory, impossible to forget. Life in its entirety was translated from actual existence into words.

After Baydaa woke up and before she had her breakfast, she picked *One Hundred Years of Solitude* off the shelf above my desk. She asked – begged first and then insisted, actually – that she be allowed to take the notebook and the novel home with her. I gave in on the condition that she return the notebook to me the following day, and that she keep the novel as a gift to remind her of our friendship.

Here is page 19 of the notebook (exactly as we read it in Baydaa's handwriting):

After graduating with a degree in science, Osama married one of his university classmates and brought her to live in his father's house in the neighbourhood. Haifa was a tall, beautiful young woman with light skin. She bore him two daughters, Mala'ika and Niran. After giving birth to the first, Haifa left her government job to look after the household. Osama was transformed, however, into a very peculiar person by the bitter days of the sanctions. He too left his job and began doing business at the market, buying and selling used furniture.

It became rare for Osama to return home before nightfall, and rare for any of us to meet him in our neighbourhood's streets. But at midnight every night, the neighbours in his alley – particularly those who lived on either side – heard the sound of continuous fighting with his wife, with whom he lived on the second floor, which opened onto the roof of the house.

Haifa submitted to his daily bouts of madness. She suffered from bouts of hysteria that would strike suddenly when copious amounts of alcohol made Osama stagger up the stairs to their bedroom. Osama's sick father often intervened to distract him from breaking the furniture; his weary mother often intervened to bring him back to his senses. But things kept going downhill as time went on. Osama's poor wife did not have family with whom she could seek refuge from this hell: they had left the country years before.

One morning, Haifa was on her way to the market when a handsome young man approached and asked her to help him find a certain house. He had the address on a piece of paper in his hand, which he held up for Haifa to read. Haifa apologised for not knowing the address and turned away, but the young man continued to follow her.

Every morning, he would be waiting for her in the same place where he had met her that first time. He would subject her to a heavy dose of flirtation, emphasising the allure of her body – specifically, her hips, her breasts and her lips. Haifa resisted all his appeals and more than once changed the route she took in order to avoid meeting him, but in those days, she began feeling her body with the palm of her hand, exploring it in front of the mirror as though it were the body of a woman she did not know. She had been neglecting this deeply alluring body for a long time, ever since her husband had begun ignoring it. She experienced a severe conflict within herself between her body's appeals, pressing upon her from every side, and the innocent personal history of this body that was now constantly aroused. In the end, desire won out, and Haifa became the secret lover of a handsome man who began making frequent appearances in the neighbourhood around that time.

One morning, Mala'ika found her mother in a somewhat different state than before. She was singing to herself as she applied make-up, dabbed a lot of perfume around her neck, and put on a revealing low-cut dress that fitted tight around her hips and bottom.

The mother left with a suitcase in which she had packed some of her clothes, without having thought too much about what she was bringing. Her young daughter followed her, unnoticed by the mother. Mala'ika saw with her own surprised eyes as her mother disappeared with a young man behind a building in the market, where she got into a taxi with him that was waiting to take them away.

Haifa disappeared without a trace and without anyone knowing her fate. Her daughter left school and began caring for her sister and her father.

Baydaa wrote this story in the pages devoted to Abu Osama. It was one that she alone knew. Nadia and I were not able to confirm its accuracy, but at the same time, we kept it in the notebook because Baydaa never lied. This notebook was the complete history of the neighbourhood, and we were obliged not to leave anyone out. When it came down to it, we were not a neighbourhood of angels.

In these pages was a long description of the house and its rooms, walls and furniture, which changed greatly after Osama became skilled in buying used furniture. There was a description of the garden and its plants, a description of Mala'ika and her sister, as well as of her grandfather and grandmother, their first appearance in the neighbourhood and the nature of their relationship with the neighbours, along with the way each one of them spoke, dressed and walked. Likewise, Baydaa dedicated numerous lines to describing Haifa's passion for her body and the way she caressed it. She avoided focusing directly on its arousing parts, but in Baydaa's magical way, she drew a tangible picture of this body in words.

Baydaa did not possess just a magical singing voice. We discovered through her writing in the notebook that her true gift manifested itself in literature. She was able – in a single night – to write the neighbourhood in the form of a novel packed with events. In it she drew places, personalities and events in an enchanting way. If I had enough time, I would read you more of her pages, for she picked out unremembered events in our neighbourhood, nearly swallowed up by forgetfulness, and with a genius touch, restored them to existence.

34

The bus that was taking us to university braked suddenly and came to a stop in the middle of the street, just in time to stop its wheels from crushing an elderly man with a wooden hand cart who was refusing to get out of the way.

'Run me over and set me free from this life! I don't want to live another day in this miserable world. Just let me die!'

The driver got out to plead with the man to step out of the road. He was in despair and wanted with all his heart to die, but after a while, he came back to his senses and was ashamed of himself. He did as the bus driver asked and pulled his cart to the pavement where he sat down and wept bitterly.

How can a man want to die and feel shame at the same time? That question occupied my mind the whole way to university. Was death not the end of everything? So why did this man still retain a little shame? Did he want to take it with him in death? Do the dead also feel shame? What good was that in the other life? I loved this elderly man and wanted to go back and listen to his story. It is my nature to love people who feel ashamed, for only with such people is it possible to come to a mutually beneficial understanding. That's because shame is the magnificent quality that makes a person human.

In our neighbourhood, we would describe the best people as being 'good and shamefaced', and whenever I came across someone who did not feel a sense of shame, I would secretly think he was dangerous and wicked. Shame is not a religious or pedagogic quality, nor is it moral principle. It is rather one of the gifts of existence that prevents us from committing travesties against the rights of other people. I loved Farouq because he felt this sense of shame deeply. His face would become red whenever he encountered some embarrassing situation. I love how he looks at the ground when talking about his father. I love how bashful he is around people when he is alone, and how he avoids the fans who admire him for being a famous football player.

What if Farouq lost this sense of shame? Would he still be the same person? What if shame evaporated suddenly from our lives – would we be transformed into a jungle? That jungle in which we were living consisted more precisely in a lack of shame that descended upon us suddenly.

I arrived at university and found Farouq waiting for me across the street from the printing shop. I walked with him to where he had parked his new car in a secluded road branching off the main street. Before he said goodbye and got in, he told me what he had been wanting to say but had been too ashamed: 'My mother and my aunt… Tomorrow at your house, they're going to seek an engagement from your family.'

'Farouq, where's this surprise coming from?'

'What do you mean, surprise?'

'It's just that I wasn't ready for this news.'

'Think about it on your own for a day,' he said, looking at the ground.

'It's not something I need to think about. You know me and how deeply I love you. But things these days – it's not really a good time for engagement and marriage.'

'Why not?'

'I don't know – my family might emigrate.'

'I'm ready to marry you in any place, in any country, on any continent. Wherever you go, I'll be right behind you.'

'That's not the point, my love. Let's just think carefully before we make a decision that isn't right.'

'Take your time, but my mother and my aunt are coming by tomorrow.'

He turned away, unhappy with my response. As he got in his car and drove off, I remained frozen on that spot and spun around trying to catch my breath. My God, what had just happened?

From a personal point of view, I was not ready for this news. I actually had not even thought about it. I had thought that we were still playing. Why did love turn into a social contract, an obligation like the homework you had to do for school?

At the same time, an obscure joy pulsed inside me, though it did not know how to break through and express itself. My heart rejoiced even as it was choked with misgivings. Every girl dreamed of marrying the boy she loved, but at the same time, marriage meant a contraction of her world, a shrinking of the dream's scope, a story coming to an end before all the chapters were written.

Love as a teenager is like young children smoking. It is the desire to move into the world of adults with a child's mouth and a grown-up cigarette. How can the child trade away his mouth for the sake of a cigarette burning between his lips?

Am I a teenager? I got past that childish nonsense long ago, and I have no desire to repeat the beautiful mistakes of the past. Am I a mature woman? I do not know.

How could I tell Farouq that I was not ready, psychologically? Would he consider that an outright refusal? How would this handsome young man, this gifted sports star, understand some girl refusing to marry him? But I was not some girl; I was his girlfriend.

I loved him. Indeed, I loved him to death. This solitary white bird in the depressing purple sky is the only thing for whom I can say that life is life and not a giant prison. I loved adolescent Farouq, playing on the neighbourhood team. I loved the Farouq in whose hands my hands planted themselves as my heart trembled beside him. That good and shamefaced young man, who released me from my shame and set me free to sing... but how could this same man be my husband?

Are love and marriage two different worlds? Two rivers flowing in opposite directions? Are we able to swim in both at the same time without drowning in one? Farouq, my love... Have you missed the goal this time and kicked the ball out of play?

That same day, without any warning, I was approached by Mundhir, who studied with me in the same department. He told me he liked me. I stammered as though I were hearing that for the first time in my life. I did not know how to respond to this eloquent young man, who was shamefaced too. I did not have it in me to ruin his day, so I gathered my positive energy and told him with perfect calm, 'I'm engaged, Mundhir.'

With this abrupt sentence, I moved from life in all its possibilities into the world of Farouq alone. I had drawn a tight circle around myself, a circle shaped like Farouq.

35

Yes, we do not cross the same river twice, but with the power of imagination, we are able to create a river of memories that flows over us thousands of times.

There is no longer a neighbourhood in our neighbourhood. Our neighbourhood has moved into the big blue notebook filled with stories and ghosts, sometimes in Nadia's handwriting, sometimes in mine, and sometimes in Baydaa's. We have written there everything that was possible to write.

The three of us are now waiting for the moment when one of our families emigrates, when we will close the record once and for all. For out of its pages come real stories sometimes, real events that we lived with all the force of their time. Its pages have become our tourist destination, where we wander without any fear. In the past, everything that could happen has already taken place, and it is not particularly important to me what exactly happened. The important thing now is what's in my head.

The anxiety begins when I think more about what is approaching in the present time, which hovers over a land made of fear, caution and watchfulness.

'Baydaa dropped out of university.' That is a real sentence that Nadia and I wrote on the page for Baydaa's family in the notebook. 'Baydaa's family is preparing to emigrate.' That is another true sentence. 'The black Chevrolet that will carry Baydaa's family far away came.' A new sentence that is also true. 'Baydaa and her family got in without saying goodbye to us. The car started to move and we shed many tears. The car set off and more tears fell. The car reached the end of the street and our tears raced to the pavement. Biryad followed the car in a daze. It made the turn and was lost from sight. Biryad returned, broken. We went inside the house and closed the door.'

This true paragraph entered our notebook all at once, but it did not tell us everything that happened exactly. What was the scene like behind the window of the car where Baydaa waved to us with the hand that wrote every story of our lives?

Did you see her face in these true sentences? Did you mark the terror in her eyes as she turned about like a bird trapped in a dark box, breathing the memories of its distant nest? Did Baydaa exit our lives and enter the record of the past, the details of which she herself recorded? Did Baydaa question her spirit on the long road to the border, on the road of tears and farewells where she took her laughter away from me and disappeared?

Baydaa, where did you go? Is this your time? Come back! I want to kiss you, to embrace you, to get my fill of you, to cry, to die of sadness in your arms. Is it true I will not see you again? What will I call my life without your presence in it?

Whatever I did not write in the record, whatever I forgot to write, that is what remains for us of our days in this place – Nadia and I, the two oldest children in the neighbourhood – our memories, our joys, our sorrow, our delights, our pains. We are all that remains of a time that melts before us like a piece of ice on the hot ground.

Nadia dropped out of university. I dropped out. She sat at home, and I sat at home. She counted up the days spent over the coals of fear, according to the number of victims of car bombs and snipers, according to the number of strangers as they painted the houses of our neighbourhood in bright colours. All this is by the grace of their Lord. As for our Lord, he has bidden us to emigrate, and I counted up the days like Nadia.

Which of the two cars would arrive before the other? Our car or that of Nadia's family? That is the one remaining question on the test, and the last person remaining in the examination hall is the one who will be able to give a final answer to this bitter question.

Nadia decided to spend the night with us in my room. She stretched out on my bed, touching everything around her. She paged through all my notebooks. She listened to all my music tapes straight through. She danced every dance she knew. She gave me a thousand kisses and petted Biryad, who spent the night with us there. She gave him a new name that remained a secret between the three of us. She kept chatting the whole time, talking without interruption. She wanted to say everything, but then the rising sun shone through the window and she had to go home.

She shed the last of her tears at the door of my bedroom. I went out with her to the gate. She took hold of my hand and started walking. An hour later, their black Chevrolet came and she got in with her family. I stood behind the gate, watching her in numb silence. Nadia was leaving me all by myself.

Was she really leaving me all alone? It is more correct to say she was abandoning a shattered object from the past. A ruined hut consumed by flames in a dark forest. A ghost of sadness with surprised eyes, a heart rent by pain and a groan that burned in my throat.

What is life? What is the neighbourhood, the street? What are memories, and what is Nadia, disappearing on the long road to the border? Listen, long road, don't you ever get tired?

I imagine her in times like this. She sits in the back seat and gives herself over to memories. I imagine that she begins from the first night we met in the shelter. No, she would begin with our time in primary school. She would think of Ahmad, and then of Marwa. She would come back to memories of me, and she would cry. She would look for her mobile phone and try to call me, but she sees that the reception is weak and her battery is running out. She would lean against the window and try to count the hills of sand along the desert road. Then she would remember me again and cry. She would sleep. Now she is dreaming, and I see her dreams. Dreams are not like telephones. Our shared dreams always connect on the network; their batteries never die.

I want to ask your forgiveness for leaving out my remaining days in Baghdad. I am embarrassed with you watching. I tried to write about a beautiful time for you, but where can I now come up with a beautiful time?

Nadia and I were born during the war with Iran. We got to know each other during Desert Storm. We grew up in the years of the sanctions and the second Gulf War. George Bush and his son, George W. Bush, took turns firing missiles and illegal weapons at our childhood, while Bill Clinton and that old woman Madeleine Albright were satisfied with starving us. And when we grew up, hell sat in wait for us.

I will trick you with my words and dodge my memories. I will sing and cry; I will dream with Nadia. I will distract myself by talking to the American pilot. I will open the neighbourhood record and choose only the happy days. I will do all that until the black Chevrolet comes and carries us across the border.

We are the last teardrop aboard the ship, the last smile, the last sigh, the last footstep on its ageing pavement. We are the last people to line their eyes with its dust. We are the ones who will tell its full story. We will tell it to neighbours' children born in foreign countries, to their grandchildren not yet born – we, the witnesses of everything that happened.

A black car stopped at our door today at dawn. On its back window, white letters read: 'By the grace of our Lord.'

We got in, and it took us away. There was no one in the street shedding tears over us apart from Biryad, whom we left behind all alone. He looked in our faces, one by one, not believing what he saw. Like a madman, he jumped up on our wall and stretched himself out like a plaster statue.

No one remained apart from him for us to wave goodbye to. We were the last of the exiles, and our house was the last of the houses that the Lord granted by his grace to others.

My heart waved to the black statue of Biryad as he raised his white tail in grief at his desolation. My heart waved at our house, our garden, the wall around them, our windows, and at a small cat jumping now from the wall to the abandoned house. Here is Ma'mun Tower. There is the destroyed Baghdad Clock. Here is the tower in Al-Zawra. The ship is ready to welcome new travellers aboard. The land does not move on with those who loved it and lived their years there. It suffers in silence and preserves them in memory.

Book II

The Future

The future: not every new thing that comes through the workings of time, but rather everything we do not know.

36

Two years ago, I discovered Nadia by chance on Instagram. I nearly died from the intensity of my joy. But unfortunately, it was a virtual joy, a joy that resembled our frozen pictures on social media. Or like our cold words in response to these sites. This was not Nadia. This was a woman who looked like her. Nadia was not married, and she did not have a small daughter. This was a woman from some other world, some other time.

This was not the same person I had met in a shelter protecting us against the air raids. It was not the same person I had lived with most of the years of my life. This man with her in the picture was not Ahmad. Some days later, we spoke by telephone. Her voice too was not Nadia's voice. Her interests were not Nadia's interests as I had known them and memorised them in my heart and in my soul.

In the virtual world, on our social media sites, discovering an old friend resembles a real event that crashes into you with all its emotional force. With the passage of time, the spark of light fades, and it gradually becomes virtual again.

The virtual world is not only a means of communication, it is a tool to examine the past and settle our accounts with it.

Day after day, I kept eluding her, this virtual Nadia. I secluded myself with my memories of her. I was afraid of her imaginary presence in our real story.

I opened the notebook containing the record of our neighbourhood and leafed through the pages. I was looking for a space to write that Nadia no longer existed. But I hesitated and closed the notebook.

When we get ready to resume old memories, we need new hearts, not used ones. Fresh hearts, in which we construct new civilisations of friendship. We write a new history upon them, a story never before told. We enter its world for the first time and get to know its protagonists for the first time too.

Has our story become just an old tale we need to fold up and put away? Do we need to write a new novel about our lives that begins where the old one left off?

Our virtual relationship gradually faded away, and the memories remained frozen in place. Whenever an old memory insisted on coming to mind, I would ignore its existence on Instagram and go to the record of the past to learn from its worlds the moments we experienced together with all that warmth.

When we left Baghdad, I took in my hand luggage *The Baghdad Clock: The Record of a Neighbourhood*. I kept it close in our house in Jordan like a secret treasure I was hiding from intrusive eyes. I opened it every now and then to read some pages that Baydaa had recorded, line by line. Through her words, I remembered the faces of our neighbours, their houses and the details of their lives. I remembered the songs they liked. I played with their children and chatted with the grandmothers. I tasted the lunches they made and I smelled the fragrance of the roses in their gardens.

One night, I opened the record and began reading with a ravenous appetite. I examined the letters and listened to the old voices from afar. Suddenly, I came across a group of strange pages, carefully folded up inside. On them, in a thick black script, were written two words: 'The Future'.

I was surprised to find these pages I had never seen before in our record of the past. Doubt nagged at me as to whether some hand was secretly reaching out to mock all my memories. But these words, 'The Future', were written in Baydaa's familiar script. They were written with the same pen that Baydaa had used when she stayed up that night to record the events of her memory, but with a darker ink, as though she had run the pen over these letters more than once.

Where had these words, 'The Future', come from then? And what were they doing here in a record of the past?

My hands trembled as I tried to touch the first pages. I hesitated a long while, and the blood ran cold in my veins. My heart was beating violently, and I nearly choked with terror at this unexpected surprise, for I had no great confidence – not even a little – in this 'future'.

How did this stranger slip into the record of the past? What was this mystery doing here? My hands kept shaking, and my forehead beaded with sweat. My mouth dried up entirely.

I left the notebook open where it was and went downstairs, leaning against the wall that ran down the staircase to the ground floor. I was parched and needed a mouthful of water. It was as though I had crossed an entire desert in a blaze of unending afternoons. I opened the refrigerator and drank three glasses of cold water, one after the other. Having quenched my thirst, I returned with heavy steps to my room.

The ghost of the future had closed the shades and turned out the lights. It began roaming throughout the room. There was a strange hand knocking on my window in the darkness. I felt like I was choking and collapsed onto my bed. I wanted to wrap myself in the blankets and sleep, but fear deprived me of the ability even to lay my head on the edge of the pillow. Dear God, what in the world was going on?

I turned on the light again. The ceiling fan was going around slowly, all on its own, drawing strange phantoms on the walls with its three blades. I gathered my strength and tiptoed back over to the record, its pages fluttering softly in the air of the fan. The ghost of the future was turning the pages of the past in front of me, smiling invisibly to itself. I recoiled to collect myself where I stood, two steps away.

A surreptitious hand reached out to open those folded pages in the record. Another hand took hold of my neck and brought my head close to the notebook. Once again, I took two steps back, my body shaking all over. But the hand on my neck forced me to return. With fingers weak from dread, I turned over the first page. I brought my eyes close to the words drawn in small, slanted letters and began to read.

Book of the Future, Page 1

I am the future. I live now in a continuous birthing from the womb of the past. Here I am on my way to you. Be calm; be not afraid. It is not only that which has occurred that has settled in the past. Do not tell anyone, I beg of you, but that which occurs in the time to come will likewise settle there too. The past rolls up the present and swallows that which is to come. It advances like a dust storm, billowing up towards the sky and blocking the horizon. No one has the power to block the storm of the past as it presses on to its end. No one has the power to push the future forward and keep it from its place.

I am here for your sake: for the sake of summarising your story; for the sake of cleansing the years and warding off any sense of tedium. Do not be afraid of me. All possible endings are still open. I will leave you to delight in their chaos, their surprises and their longed-for outcomes. The future is a theatre of suspense, the secret factory that produces all that is unexpected.

I do not want to ruin your life. I have some joyful news, news that you would consider happy, and I also have some painful realities. I am sorry to bring them, but from a different perspective, they are unavoidable if you want the good news to bring any joy.

What is the use of happiness that does not dawn after the long night of pain? How beautiful is the rain when it bursts unexpectedly from the heart of a storm to clean the dust from the air! So that you will be glad about a good future, join me in skipping page two, and start reading on page three. When you reach page six, leave it folded as it is, both it and page seven as well. Take up the page coming next – page eight, I mean. Continue reading until the beginning of the ten pages right before the end, and stop there immediately. Do not read the last pages. Leave them folded just as they are. I warn you not to approach them, and I urge you follow my instructions to the letter. Just as I want to caution you that I am not like the past in its rigidity and its decisiveness regarding objects, realities and events. Being the future, I am ruled by my nature, by fits of sharp temper and by a rapid shift from state to state.

What is written in my pages is not put down in permanent ink. My pages are composed in light and shadow. One effaces the other depending on the conditions and according to ability, desire and temperament.

Are you feeling reassured towards me now?

Have the fear, hesitation and anxiety left you?

I advise you now to go to bed. I will leave you to sleep in the most tranquil peace and comfort. Tomorrow morning, when the sun rises in the east and light comes through the window, eat your breakfast and drink a cup of tea. Open the notebook once again and begin to read naturally, without shrinking back or becoming emotional, just as though you were reading an exciting new novel devised by the imagi-nation of a crazy author, and not a completion of the past that picks up where your old book, *The Baghdad Clock: The Record of a Neighbourhood*, leaves off.

And since you do not dream, I cannot wish you sweet dreams. I will content myself with saying, sleep well, you good and pure creature.

*

After I finished reading the letter from the future, I calmly got up, went straight to my bed and slept.

The next morning, I woke in a different mood. I took a relaxing bath. Tuning the radio to a classical music station, I opened my windows to the sunshine, and ate breakfast. I sat down and serenely began turning over the pages permitted to me, free from fear.

Book of the Future, Page 3:

Uncle Shawkat and Baji Nadira

Despite the repeated urging of Baji Nadira, Uncle Shawkat insisted on not selling their old house in the neighbourhood.

'My dear husband, no one we know is going back there. Things have changed. Life has changed. Everything is now gone.'

But after all her pleading, Uncle Shawkat declared that, as far as he was concerned, everything would eventually go back to normal. Every spring evening, when he sat with her in the garden of their house in the centre of Sulaymaniyah, he would recall for her beautiful memories of their lives in the neighbourhood. He told her about Baghdad: its beauty, its magic and its golden days. He would talk to her about Al-Rashid Street and the Orosdi Back department store, or about River Street and how he bought her wedding dress there. He told her about the Tigris, about Abu Nuwas Street and the fancy neighbourhoods of Al-Mansur and Al-Mu'min, about his idyllic childhood in the time of the monarchy, about his business studies in secondary school, and later on in the College of Economics.

He told her about his job in the central bank and about the arc of the Iraqi dinar. He told her things she knew well and had experienced personally alongside him, but he still loved to tell them, just as though he were getting to know her for the first time. Every time his imagination went to the past, he took her left hand and, with utmost tenderness, used his anxious teeth to press the trace of a watch on her wrist.

Baji Nadira would say, 'We've grown old, dear husband. There's no hope of a new life in Baghdad again. Let's sell the house and use the proceeds to buy a large grave in the cemetery on the mountain. We'll ask in our will that they erect a small room over it, on the walls of which they write the story of our love, from the first day we met until the last day of our lives.'

At that, Uncle Shawkat would stare into space for a while and reply, 'Everything will go back to normal.'

When the evening cold fell in the garden, Baji Nadira would take her husband by the hand and bring him inside. He was sick, and could no longer endure the mild spring breezes. She would sit with him, watching television, and in less than an hour, when he closed his eyes, she would cover him up and go to her bed.

Biryad would appear in Uncle Shawkat's dreams, rushing down the side of a towering mountain. Biryad would start rolling towards him like a black rock that came to a halt by crashing into the front of his shoes.

Book of the Future, Page 4:

Hussam, the brother of Mayada

After murdering his sister and escaping to Jordan, Hussam left roughly a year later for a different country on the border, where he changed his name to Abu Sayf and became a political opponent to the dictatorial regime in Iraq. Immediately after the regime's fall, he returned to Baghdad with a thick beard and black sunglasses that he wore all the time. He became a member of the first parliament formed after independence, and then an important official in an executive government agency.

One dark night, he went out and entered the neighbourhood in a long procession of black armoured cars. He ordered his followers to close off its roads with concrete barriers, and he blocked its entrances with fences of barbed wire. He put a black mark on all the abandoned houses. Then he began selling them, one by one, on the pretence that they were the ancestral property of his family.

When he went inside his family's old house, he began to examine his memories. His sister Mayada rose from her sleep in the dark. She approached him, her feet leaving footsteps in the dust on the tiles.

'Why? Why did you kill me?'

Terrified and not believing his eyes, Hussam took a step back. After some moments of distraction and anxiety, he confirmed that this young woman in front of him was his sister Mayada in flesh and blood, in the same clothes that had been stained with blood the day of the crime, her hair done up the same way. The voice he heard was her same voice. No one can say how long he remained frozen there, in that place. Meanwhile, her eyes sank into his soul like a sharp knife through soft clay. He tried to break himself away and call his bodyguard, but he had no voice. He tried to move, but his feet were stuck to the tiles like an iron statue set into solid concrete.

Mayada remained where she was, watching him, motionless. And Hussam remained held by her gaze, shattered with fear. When his bodyguard realised he was taking longer than expected in a dark, abandoned house, they became worried and went inside with their flashlights. They found him dead where he stood.

The men tried to carry Hussam out, but his feet remained firmly fixed to the floor tiles. Using hammers and pickaxes, they broke apart his feet and the lower half his legs, such that he fell where he stood like a rotten tree. After loading him in the back of a pickup truck, they buried him in a deep crater made by an American bomb that had missed its target and fallen in a field, it being the closest abandoned space they happened across on their way. Minutes, hours and days instantly rained down upon his grave – the same number of minutes, hours and days since he committed his crime and murdered Mayada until the moment he was covered by the dirt.

After Mayada felt assured that time had brought her justice, she stretched out in her eternal chamber and resumed dreaming of Dr Tawfiq, who remains a bachelor to this day. She dreams the same, familiar dream: a small house, colourful curtains, simple furniture, and little ones who put on their backpacks and head off for school in the morning as she stands in the doorway, smiling and blowing a kiss to say goodbye.

Before he died, Abu Sayf had sold all the houses. He sold the entire neighbourhood, even its schools, its clinics, its shelters, its shops, its bakeries and its pharmacies. His family's old house was the only one that remained, haunted by ghosts, and in its empty rooms can be heard a voice singing the old songs that Mayada used to dance to.

Hussam's father died, as did his mother, in a terrorist attack. They had left for a distant province two months before Baghdad fell and were killed on their way back to the neighbourhood.

Book of the Future, Page 5:

Farouq and Marwa

Marwa was born on the first day of February, the same day Farouq was born, as well as you and Nadia. That day, by the way, was a prodigious one for births, when the neighbourhood welcomed the second generation of its descendants.

Marwa and her family emigrated to the United States after they obtained asylum on account of her work as a translator for the Marines. The lives of her family had been exposed to danger in Baghdad on more than one occasion.

On the way to their new country, they stayed in Jordan for several weeks. Marwa encountered Farouq there by chance and they began to meet regularly. She wanted him to deliver a letter to Ahmad from her, and in turn, he wanted her to send you his telephone number. After she left Jordan, she got in touch with him from America, and a new relationship grew between them, one that developed into a kind of love.

Farouq suffered a serious leg injury. He never regained his former level of play and was unable to join the national team. It was then that he decided to get engaged to Marwa and marry her. He moved to join her in her new country, but before too long, they separated. Farouq returned to Baghdad to work as a coach for the club in which his star had shone when he was first starting out. Before long, he emigrated a second time to the US, where he acquired citizenship. This time, however, he chose to settle down in a state far from Marwa's. At this point, he lives with an Arab girlfriend who was born in America, and he works as an assistant coach for an obscure American club. Meanwhile, Marwa married the son of a prominent Iraqi politician, to whom she bore a son. Farouq never forgot his love for you, but he was embarrassed by your abrupt response to his proposal, and his embarrassment was all the greater in front of his mother and aunt, whom he prevented from visiting your family after informing them that you were not ready.

Book of the Future, Page 8:

Baydaa, after the moment of her departure

Baydaa was born on the first day of February, the first child of parents who had got to know each other on the train going from Basra to Baghdad. Her father was a young officer in the army who was making the trip one day on leave from the front. Her mother was a doctor who had recently graduated and had received her placement to work in a village clinic near to the port city of Umm Qasr. A loving relationship developed between them, and they got married.

Baydaa had one brother, who lives with their grandmother on their mother's side. That grandmother was devoted to him from birth, and he has remained in her house to this day.

Baydaa grew up in the neighbourhood, and she went to the same school as you. You have the rest of the story, and there is no need to go over it again because, as you know, my task is not the past but rather the future, and the future does not only mean that which is yet to come in time, but also those things that happened in the past, yet which we do not know.

Never forget that everything we do not remember is the stuff of the future.

After the car transporting Baydaa's family crossed the border, the tension melted from their faces. They heaved a deep sigh of relief because Baydaa's father was travelling with falsified documents, containing a different name and profession. He had altered a passport so that it bore his photo and someone else's name underneath.

Baydaa opened the novel, *One Hundred Years of Solitude,* which you had given her. Her eye fell upon the passage in which the people of Macondo were astonished when they saw the large festival and found their village had been thrown into confusion.

A tear fell from her eye and rolled quickly down her cheek as she thought of the neighbourhood, remembering you and Nadia and how she was leaving the two of you behind to be devoured by the desolation. The neighbourhood would condense into a sphere around you and bottle up the old air in your lungs.

After leaving Baghdad, Baydaa completed her studies in their new city. Her mother found work in a new hospital, and the son of one of her colleagues proposed to Baydaa. Two months after the wedding celebration, Baydaa emigrated with her husband to Canada. There she gave birth to a beautiful daughter, whom she named after you in honour of your friendship. She also gave birth to a baby boy, whom she named Shawkat to honour the memory of Uncle Shawkat, whom she had loved. From time to time, she would touch the spot on her wrist where he would use his teeth to leave the imprint of a watch.

These days, Baydaa is free to devote herself to the house and the children. She previously felt a great desire to fulfil her dream of setting up a website that would contain the full history of the neighbourhood found in the record. She tried to contact you and Nadia but could not find your addresses. After a frustrating search, she gave it up for a while and then forgot the whole idea.

At dawn on one of those bitterly cold Canadian mornings, Baydaa got up from bed and decided to write a long novel about the small Canadian city in which she lived with her husband and their two children. Without any forethought or planning, she sat at her new computer and began to write.

I do not know what the ground looks like, encased as it is by ice. Nor the colour of the grass that used to cover it. But I know that I am born anew on the ground of this white continent, so far beyond the ocean. I do not remember how I arrived here, nor the country from which I set out. I just woke one morning and found myself enveloped by the vast whiteness, this enormous eraser that covers the face of life and sweeps away every trace of old memories in the soul.

The person born after a quarter of a century of life, finding herself in a strange geography, a strange air and a strange language, needs to forget her umbilical cord immediately, along with the womb in which she dwelt all the years preceding her new birth, just as the infant forgets the womb in which he lived before being born. From the moment of existence in this world, it is a person's nature not to remember the first womb in which he lived. He always receives the world without memory, just as if he came from nothingness. I am the new child in this world, coming from nothingness. I will tell you the story of my first day.

Baydaa finished her novel and left it to sleep on a small shelf in the living room of her apartment. She returned to it every now and then for the pleasure of reading it. At one and the same time, she was the author and the sole reader. When a person writes only for himself it means he writes in complete freedom, a feeling that professional writers never enjoy. Baydaa wrote a novel for herself, and she left it on a small shelf in the living room of her apartment.

This is the most important part of her news, and in the folded pages, the ones I warned you not to read, there are other matters that it is not important to peruse. I caution you once again against opening them, or even thinking about it: seeing what has not yet happened would make your life a living hell.

Book of the Future, Page 9:

Nadia, after the moment of departure

In a traditional family marriage, Nadia's father had married a first cousin without any preceding love story. Nadia was born on the first day of February, the second child in the family after her brother, Muayad.

You know the story of her childhood from the time of the air-raid shelter up until the last tear that fell from your eyes as you waved goodbye.

Nadia reached Damascus with her family on the night of the city's first snowfall that year. The vast, awe-inspiring whiteness was the only thing that prevented her from bursting into tears – that, and her memories of you, which kept watch over her throughout the long hours of the journey.

As is the case with most of the young women across all times that we know, Nadia automatically associated anything pure white with the wedding night. From the first moment of that snowfall, she started dreaming of marrying Ahmad, for he was still the young man she loved, with whom she had lived her first story of passionate young love. He now represented for her the entire sky of the past with its familiar birds, all things beautiful that she had left behind in the neighbourhood. In her mind, he was you, Farouq, Baydaa,

Uncle Shawkat, Abu Nabil's shop, Al-Zawra Park and the Baghdad Clock. He was the streets and alleys, the storefronts, the gardens and trees, the birds, the doors and windows. Ahmad was the entirety of the past, as well as the present she was seeking.

In the first days after her family arrived in Damascus, they rented a small apartment in a working-class district. Nadia would sit on a small balcony that extended from the front of the building to watch life in the street, as though she hoped by chance to catch Ahmad's shadow. Days passed without her hearing anything about him, but she was certain that he was present with her in the same city. Her heart told her he was close, even if she did not see him.

She opened a Facebook page, another on Instagram, and began searching for his name, sometimes in Arabic and sometimes in English. When she gave up on the virtual world, she decided to enrol at university to continue her studies. Perhaps she would come across him that way, or else find someone who could lead her to him. At the very least, she hoped to hear some news about him that would ease her anxiety. And in fact, someone did come who brought her this news:

'Ahmad got married a few days ago to a friend of his from the University of Mosul, the same friend who appeared with him in the photo he sent you when he was still a student there.'

This news fell upon Nadia's head like a thunderbolt. At first, she did not believe the girl who brought it, who happened to be the same one who brought Ahmad's letter and photo the last time, when Nadia had been studying at the University of Baghdad.

This girl had been a student there with Nadia, and her sister was studying with Ahmad at the University of Mosul.

Nadia was unable to control her emotions in front of this messenger of misery, whom fate had used to convey the worst news of her life on two separate occasions, first in Baghdad and now in Damascus. Without looking her in the eye or saying goodbye, Nadia turned around and walked away, choked by tears.

Nadia left her studies at the university and lived in painful solitude in the small apartment with her family. She would spend her days listening to old love songs that filled her spirit as memories that made her cry.

A year after this incident, a handsome young man, who worked as a civil engineer in a prominent company in Dubai, came to ask for her hand in marriage. She agreed, and a few weeks after the marriage ceremony, they departed together. She lived some beautiful days with him, all the sweeter after the birth of a lovely daughter she named Baydaa in memory of her friend.

But in recent times, she has become consumed by jealousy over her husband, constantly fearing that he will leave her, to such a degree that discomfort is his primary emotion around her. Nadia is now addicted to searching his phone ten times a day. She has developed a repulsively keen sense of smell by sniffing through his clothes for any trace of women's perfume. She watches him with a restless, tormented eye, even when he is sitting in front of the television. This is in addition to the times she calls him at work, with or without any apparent reason, just to confirm that he belongs to her alone.

Book of the Future, Page 10:

The life of Biryad

Was Biryad something in one of Nadia's dreams?

Maybe he was a bicycle tyre that became bored of turning in the dream and left. Or else let him be the clock that stayed behind in her old dream but stopped telling the time and departed. Maybe the cow, the sheep, the tree, the pillow, or anything. But most likely he was something from one of her dreams, something that, by his own wish, left, only to find himself locked inside a house. He was able to get out of the dream easily enough, but then he was caught in the maze of a large house with all its doors and windows locked. It was Umm Ali's house in the time after her family emigrated.

Hunger and thirst nearly killed him. He submitted to his fate and stretched out on the floor, waiting for the end. He was surprised when a strange man came in and brought him food and water, caring for him and giving him a new name. That man was Uncle Shawkat.

As you recall, in the very minute that the car carrying you to Jordan turned to leave, Biryad jumped up on the wall around your house. He spent the night there. He had no desire to do anything. He decided to give up food and water in order to die on that wall.

Biryad talked to himself a long while that night. He wondered about his fate, about his past and his future, about his life after death, and whether he would meet you there.

He remembered all of you; he remembered the entire neighbourhood from the day he appeared until the moment he was abandoned there.

He truly was alone. The friendly cats did not approach him. The cheerful bats did not swoop in to startle him.

How did you enter the dream, he asked himself, and why did you leave it? Why did I find myself in a house with locked doors?

Biryad got up in the morning and jumped down. He circled the houses, remembering their families. The strangers who were the new residents drove him away and shut their doors in his face. Even the children did not love him; they threw stones at him and other sharp, heavy things. His head was gashed by more than one deep cut, and his back bled from the painful blows of sticks that some of them used to drive him away mercilessly.

In the end, he decided to die. But he did not know how to do that. He cut himself off from food and water, but that became his natural state, and he no longer felt hunger or thirst. What he did feel, deeply, was the loss of respect, the shame and the insults. He did not like the cats feeling sorry for him, nor the bats, and he began avoiding their glances.

Biryad suffered a cruel blow to his right eye. A heavy flow of blood ran down far enough that he could reach it with his tongue. A child had hit him with a big rock that suddenly made the earth spin beneath him until he could no longer stand from the dizziness. Exhausted, he dragged himself away until he stretched out along the wall of your house. Some little children were following him and began pelting him with handfuls of pebbles. Biryad rose heavily to his feet and plodded towards the main street. He stood there for a while, watching the cars race past, and when a large truck came by, he rolled under its wheels and ended his life.

Book of the Future, Page 11:

Happy News

Less than a year from now, you too will marry an exceptionally nice young man who graduated from a prestigious international university. He will appear in your life suddenly, meeting you by chance in the street on a visit to his family, which lives next to yours in Jordan. In that moment, he will say to himself, 'This is the girl I've been dreaming of my whole life.' At the end of the weekend, he will walk up with a red rose and tell you, 'I like you,' and when you hesitate in your reply, he will say, 'I love you.'

The two of you will get married and head off to live in Dubai too.

Is this happy news, as far as you are concerned?

Do not reply too quickly: more happy news is still on the way. Now get up and relax a little. Drink a cup of tea or coffee, listen to a song from the recent past, something from your days in the neighbourhood. Wander among your memories there, and then come along with me.

The future organises its pages well. It makes additions and abbreviations; it erases and corrects, cuts and pastes. The future is more flexible than the past. The past that you love cannot bend at all. Do not say yet again, 'Everything that could happen in the past has actually happened.' That is not true in the least. What would it mean to live only that which we know and are used to, without any surprises or disappointed expectations? That would make life a prison of memory revolving around itself for evermore.

✱

I gently closed the notebook. Getting up, I drew back the curtain to let the sunshine into the room. I made a cup of tea. I listened to a song I loved by Haitham Yousif. It begins with a long introduction in that organ music so familiar from the nineties, and a melody so sweet it squeezes my soul.

I stood in front of the mirror and looked at my face. I saw him there in the depths, standing behind me: that handsome and elegant young man who holds a red rose and comes up to say with all the warmth in the world, 'I love you.'

'I love you too.'

✱

Do not tell me this is the least of your concerns. No, it is of the utmost importance, my beautiful one. Do not run away from your femininity. Do not shatter it with lies. Do not suppress the voice of the woman that is inside you. Do not slap down your desires simply because you are liberated and cultured. Do not betray yourself. Do not invalidate the needs you have put on hold. Do not stray far from your body. Do not keep your distance from the song of womanhood that wants to express itself.

The dream of the white dress does not keep you from being cultured, liberated and strong. Dream for the sake of the tenderness found inside your soul. Dream of the wedding night, of the music, of the first dance. Eat the cake from his hand, and feed him from yours. Enfold him in your arms and dance with him like a princess in a fairy tale.

Be cultured and liberated and strong, but let love come from the right place, at the right time. It comes with a red rose, the touch of a hand, a kiss.

Do not block the river in the waterway. Do not pour concrete over the sparrow's nest. Do not keep the sunshine from stealing inside your darkened room.

*

When I finished talking to my image in the mirror, I went back to my place and sat at the table once again. I opened the *Book of the Future* where I had left off and resumed reading.

*

Your wedding reception will be a historic event never to be forgotten, neither in your life, nor in the lives of your family members, nor in the lives of anyone who loves you and shares your life. He loves you, and for your sake, he will prepare surprises you cannot imagine, things that never would have occurred to you, that you never dreamed of – because after all, you do not dream.

After you cut the wedding cake, and after you dance to the music of a beautiful song you love, but before you return to your seats, new music will begin playing in the music hall, and with it, a sudden trilling and shouting will burst out, voices talking over each other, a general chaos of whistling together with vigorous, uninterrupted applause. In a dazzling moment, you will turn towards where the band is playing. A sudden light blinds you. You close your eyes and open them to see Kathem Al-Saher.

*

I rubbed my eyes and began reading again. I held the page in the book carefully and turned it over to make sure I was reading the future section. Then I got up, turned around a few times, opened the window, and began speaking to the birds, the trees and the air: 'Kathem Al-Saher?!'

Leave off, O Book of the Future! Stop for a while. Let me talk to you for a few minutes. In your kindness, give me leave to state what you do not know, what you are not thinking of because it has not occurred to you.

Kathem Al-Saher is not just a talented and successful singer-songwriter, not just a dazzling poet. This is not the full story of Kathem Al-Saher as far as we are concerned – my generation, that is, which experienced sadness, frustration and failure on every side. Kathem was a bright light shining in the dark sky, a unique success that seemed miraculous at a time when everything was collapsing around us.

Kathem Al-Saher: a deep question in our exam book, and a confusing answer on the question sheet. How did this young man escape the grip of those bitter days when time ran backwards? How did he sail his small boat through the ocean of stormy terrors that completely devastated our lives? The entire world stood at the door of our house to prevent our success. The entire earth spun us through the air of failure, and in those cruel years, Kathem Al-Saher was writing a success story. Life pushed us towards non-existence, and Kathem brought us to centre stage.

I am not talking here about the romantic Kathem Al-Saher, whose songs have made millions of people happy, and about whom millions of girls dreamed. I am talking about the success story itself. Do you know, O Future, what it means to succeed, when you are prevented from even entering the examination hall? Do you know what it means that people see you in a song, and it becomes your entire essence?

I return to the notebook and reread the last lines. I hear Kathem Al-Saher's song at my wedding reception:

Fold me upon your chest and take me away from them all

A colourful bouquet of roses appears in my hand, I take two steps towards the centre of the hall and lose myself in a long dance. My white gown changes into a flock of small white gulls that circle the hall and then fly out of the window to the distant sky.

Book of the Future, Page 12:

The Baghdad Clock

The clock stopped at six minutes and forty seconds past five in the morning, when the Americans bombed it and destroyed the building on which it stood so tall. All the contents of the museum inside were looted within a month of its being destroyed. The minutes flowed away from the clock hands onto the ground and time stopped altogether.

Years later, the government resolved to restore the clock so that it might stand again with its four faces. As it happened, each of these four clocks pointed to a different time. So you could say, for example, that it is seven in the morning, local Baghdad time. Meanwhile, somebody on the opposite side would say, 'It is five in the afternoon, local Baghdad time.' On a third side, a person passing through the city by chance could say, 'It's now two in the afternoon on Wednesday, the ninth of April 2003.' Simultaneously and without any mistake, somebody else standing not far away on the side facing him could say, 'The time is now four in the morning on Sunday, the tenth of February in the year 1258.'

Thus the local time in a single city was confused, and its people were divided according to the position from which they looked at the clock. In this prodigious city, different generations coexisted without having a natural feeling for the time in which they lived.

People began swimming through time, mistaking remote centuries for recent years. It became possible to see Nebuchadnezzar and Samir Amin sitting in a restaurant where Yazdegerd III worked as a waiter. Harun al-Rashid in military garb presented Charlemagne with an hourglass that fell to the ground and shattered; a street cleaner came and swept it away. Meanwhile the Abbasid caliph Al-Mu'tadid Bi-llah hurried past the restaurant window with a bomb, on his way to destroy the statue of General Maude. When he passed the famous Arab traveller, Ibn Jubayr, the latter wrote these lines in his noted book, *The Travels*:

> Even if it is still the capital of the Abbasid Caliphate and the gathering place of the Qurayshi tribe, the form of this ancient city has departed, and only its name remains. Beyond the dilapidated ruins or the statue of a towering horseman – that which it used to be prior to these events that have rained upon it, before the eyes of misfortune turned this way – there is no beauty here that might arrest the gaze. It invites the active mind to careless contemplation. The only exception is its Tigris River, lying between the workshops and jetties like a polished mirror in a dull frame or a woven necklace under the collarbone. Indeed, we return to it, and we do not thirst; we stare into it like a burnished mirror that does not rust.

Ibn Jubayr recorded these words and set about counting the burning buildings along Al-Rashid Street, in Al-Saadun Street, and down Abu Nuwas Street. Then he sat at the statue of Ali Baba and the Forty Thieves and began to write:

> When time was the receptacle into which life was poured, only to gush forth again in a flowing succession divided

by hours and minutes, the people in the city of Baghdad became diametrically opposed in their creeds, their views, their clothing and hair, their taste in food and drink, and their sleeping, sitting, walking and standing.

Some, when they found it difficult to adjust to this epochal chaos, decided of their own free will to go and live in the past. They decided to open Al-Tabari's *History* and insert themselves into its pages and become historical figures. They wore shabby scraps of clothing and revived the turbans of old. They grew their beards down to their chests. At certain times, they massacred people who did not resemble them, or they would blow themselves up in social gatherings, yelling, '*Allahu Akbar.*' Other times, they would drag people off to the slaughterhouse to butcher them like animals.

On all sides of the Baghdad Clock, the same historical battles were renewed, and many people died. The Caliph of Death appeared on the back of an iron mount in a column of beasts stretching from Raqqa in Syria to the antiquities of Nimrod. He wore a broken Rolex watch on his wrist in order to proclaim that his time had come. He killed everyone he met along the path of his procession – men, women and children. He razed walls, dried out rivers, uprooted trees and buried gardens. The caliph and the crime become a single thing, and death became the song of that obscene time, the time of *Allahu Akbar*, announced by innocent blood butchered on the hills of Iraq.

Epilogue

I know I was a dream in someone's head. And I know I will live in Dubai. I know I will work here in this city, where I will establish a new life out of a used past. I know Nadia lives in Dubai too and that we will resume our friendship in its entirety, with its deep roots and its memories. She will spend the night at my place, and I will spend the night at hers. I will go to see her each day, and she will visit me. I know that my life and hers have been tied together by a fate that cannot be shaken. The madness of history tears us apart; geography brings us together.

Here I am on my way to see her, caught in traffic and remembering. I will be at her place in minutes. Her daughter will welcome me at the door of the house, and she will cling to me just as her mother did once in the shelter when we were small, when we sought protection from death and shared our dreams.

I do not need the *Book of the Future* to know all this. But what I do not know is that which the hand of days has recorded in the forbidden pages, the events sleeping in those lines that the future warned me not to approach.

Will I ignore these warnings and draw near?

Why do we fear our final destinies?

What if we knew that which the unknown keeps hidden from us? How would anything change unless we also knew the paths that led us there?

I do not know!

The events of this novel, the neighbourhood and its characters, the narrator and her friends and her life, have all proceeded from dreams and imagination that have sought to take their place in the world of reality.

About the Author

Shahad Al Rawi was born in Baghdad in 1986. She is a writer and novelist. Her first novel *The Baghdad Clock* went through three printings in the first months of publication. She is currently completing a PhD in Anthropology in Dubai.

About the Translator

Luke Leafgren received his PhD in Comparative Literature from Harvard University in 2012, after taking BA degrees in English and theology from Columbia University and the University of Oxford. He has translated several Arabic novels into English and teaches Arabic at the University of Harvard, where he also serves as assistant dean of Harvard College. He is an avid sailor and designed the StandStand portable standing desk.

Oneworld, Many Voices

Bringing you exceptional writing
from around the world

The Unit by Ninni Holmqvist (Swedish)
Translated by Marlaine Delargy

Twice Born by Margaret Mazzantini (Italian)
Translated by Ann Gagliardi

Things We Left Unsaid by Zoya Pirzad (Persian)
Translated by Franklin Lewis

The Space Between Us by Zoya Pirzad (Persian)
Translated by Amy Motlagh

The Hen Who Dreamed She Could Fly by Sun-mi Hwang
(Korean) Translated by Chi-Young Kim

The Hilltop by Assaf Gavron (Hebrew)
Translated by Steven Cohen

Morning Sea by Margaret Mazzantini (Italian)
Translated by Ann Gagliardi

A Perfect Crime by A Yi (Chinese)
Translated by Anna Holmwood

The Meursault Investigation by Kamel Daoud (French)
Translated by John Cullen

Minus Me by Ingelin Røssland (YA) (Norwegian)
Translated by Deborah Dawkin

Laurus by Eugene Vodolazkin (Russian)
Translated by Lisa C. Hayden

Masha Regina by Vadim Levental (Russian)
Translated by Lisa C. Hayden

French Concession by Xiao Bai (Chinese)
Translated by Chenxin Jiang

The Sky Over Lima by Juan Gómez Bárcena (Spanish)
Translated by Andrea Rosenberg

A Very Special Year by Thomas Montasser (German)
Translated by Jamie Bulloch

Umami by Laia Jufresa (Spanish)
Translated by Sophie Hughes

The Hermit by Thomas Rydahl (Danish)
Translated by K.E. Semmel

The Peculiar Life of a Lonely Postman by Denis Thériault
(French) Translated by Liedewy Hawke

Three Envelopes by Nir Hezroni (Hebrew)
Translated by Steven Cohen

Fever Dream by Samanta Schweblin (Spanish)
Translated by Megan McDowell

The Postman's Fiancée by Denis Thériault (French)
Translated by John Cullen

The Invisible Life of Euridice Gusmao by Martha Batalha
(Brazilian Portuguese) Translated by Eric M. B. Becker

The Temptation to Be Happy by Lorenzo Marone
(Italian) Translated by Shaun Whiteside

Sweet Bean Paste by Durian Sukegawa (Japanese)
Translated by Alison Watts

They Know Not What They Do by Jussi Valtonen (Finnish)
Translated by Kristian London

The Tiger and the Acrobat by Susanna Tamaro (Italian)
Translated by Nicoleugenia Prezzavento and Vicki Satlow

The Woman at 1,000 Degrees by Hallgrímur Helgason
(Icelandic) Translated by Brian FitzGibbon

Frankenstein in Baghdad by Ahmed Saadawi (Arabic)
Translated by Jonathan Wright

Back Up by Paul Colize (French)
Translated by Louise Rogers Lalaurie

Damnation by Peter Beck (German)
Translated by Jamie Bulloch

Oneiron by Laura Lindstedt (Finnish)
Translated by Owen Witesman

The Boy Who Belonged to the Sea by Denis Thériault
(French) Translated by Liedewy Hawke

The Baghdad Clock by Shahad Al Rawi (Arabic)
Translated by Luke Leafgren

The Aviator by Eugene Vodolazkin (Russian)
Translated by Lisa C. Hayden

Lala by Jacek Dehnel (Polish)
Translated by Antonia Lloyd-Jones